SIDNEY SHELDON is the author of *The Other Side of Midnight*, *A Stranger in the Mirror*, *Bloodline*, *Rage of Angels*, *Master of the Game*, *If Tomorrow Comes*, *Windmills of the Gods*, *The Sands of Time*, *Memories of Midnight*, *The Doomsday Conspiracy*, *The Stars Shine Down*, *Nothing Lasts Forever*, *Morning, Noon & Night* and *The Best Laid Plans*, all number one international bestsellers. His first book, *The Naked Face*, was acclaimed by the *New York Times* as 'the best first mystery novel of the year'. Mr Sheldon has won a Tony Award for Broadway's *Redhead* and an Academy Award for *The Bachelor and the Bobby Soxer*. *Rage of Angels*, *Master of the Game*, *Windmills of the Gods* and *Memories of Midnight* have been made into highly successful television miniseries.

He has written the screenplays for twenty-three motion pictures including *Easter Parade* (with Judy Garland) and *Annie Get Your Gun*. He also created four long-running television series, including *Hart to Hart* and *I Dream of Jeannie*, which he produced. He was awarded the 1993 Prix Littéraire de Deauville, from the Deauville Film Festival, and is now included in the Guiness Book of Records as 'The Most Translated Author.' Mr Sheldon and his wife live in southern California and London.

SIDNEY SHELDON

The Naked Face

HarperCollins*Publishers*

Harper*CollinsPublishers*
77–85 Fulham Palace Road
Hammersmith, London, W6 8JB

www.harpercollins.co.uk

First Published in Great Britain by
Hodder & Stoughton Ltd 1971

Fifth impression 2011

Copyright © Sidney Sheldon 1970

Sidney Sheldon asserts the moral right to
be identified as the author of this work

A catalogue record for this book
is available from the British Library

ISBN-13: 978-0-00-725391-3

Typeset in Sabon by Palimpsest Book Production Limited,
Polmont, Strilingshire

Printed and bound in India by
Thomson Press (I) Ltd

HarperCollins*Publishers*
A-53, Sector 57, NOIDA, Uttar Pradesh - 201301, India
77-85 Fulham Palace Road, London W6 8JB, United Kingdom
Hazelton Lanes, 55 Avenue Road, Suite 2900, Toronto, Ontario M5R 3L2
and 1995 Markham Road, Scarborough, Ontario M1B 5M8, Canada
25 Ryde Road, Pymble, Sydney, NSW 2073, Australia
31 View Road, Glenfield, Auckland 10, New Zealand
10 East 53rd Street, New York NY 10022, USA

To the Women in my Life –
Jorja
Mary
– and –
Natalie

Chapter One

At ten minutes before eleven in the morning, the sky exploded into a carnival of white confetti that instantly blanketed the city. The soft snow turned the already frozen streets of Manhattan to grey slush and the icy December wind herded the Christmas shoppers towards the comfort of their apartments and homes.

On Lexington Avenue the tall, thin man in the yellow rain slicker moved along with the rushing Christmas crowd to a rhythm of his own. He was walking rapidly, but it was not with the frantic pace of the other pedestrians who were trying to escape the cold. His head was lifted and he seemed oblivious to the passers-by who bumped against him. He was free after a lifetime of purgatory, and he was on his way home to tell Mary that it was finished. The past was going to bury its dead and the future was bright and golden. He was thinking how her face would glow when he told her the news. As he reached the corner of Fifty-ninth Street, the traffic light ambered its way to red and he stopped with the impatient crowd. A few feet away, a Salvation Army Santa Claus stood over a large kettle. The man reached in his pocket for some coins, an offering to the gods of fortune. At that instant someone clapped him on the back, a sudden stinging blow that rocked his whole body. Some overhearty Christmas drunk trying to be friendly.

Or Bruce Boyd. Bruce, who had never known his own strength and had a childish habit of hurting him physically. But he had not seen Bruce in more than a year. The man started to turn his head to see who had hit him, and to his surprise, his knees began to buckle. In slow motion, watching himself from a distance, he could see his body hit the sidewalk. There was a dull pain in his back and it began to spread. It became hard to breathe. He was aware of a parade of shoes moving past his face as though animated with a life of their own. His cheek began to feel numb from the freezing sidewalk. He knew he must not lie there. He opened his mouth to ask someone to help him, and a warm, red river began to gush out and flow into the melting snow. He watched in dazed fascination as it moved across the sidewalk and ran down into the gutter. The pain was worse now, but he didn't mind it so much because he suddenly remembered his good news. He was free. He was going to tell Mary that he was free. He closed his eyes to rest them from the blinding whiteness of the sky. The snow began to turn to icy sleet, but he no longer felt anything.

Chapter Two

Carol Roberts heard the sounds of the reception door opening and closing and the men walking in, and before she even looked up, she could smell what they were. There were two of them. One was in his middle forties. He was a big mother, about six foot three, and all muscle. He had a massive head with deep-set steely blue eyes and a weary, humourless mouth. The second man was younger. His features were clean-cut, sensitive. His eyes were brown and alert. The two men looked completely different and yet, as far as Carol was concerned, they could have been identical twins.

They were fuzz. That was what she had smelled. As they moved towards her desk she could feel the drops of perspiration begin to trickle down her armpits through the shield of anti-perspirant. Frantically her mind darted over all the treacherous areas of vulnerability. Chick? Christ, he had kept out of trouble for over six months. Since that night in his apartment when he had asked her to marry him and had promised to quit the gang.

Sammy? He was overseas in the Air Force, and if anything had happened to her brother, they would not have sent these two mothers to break the news. No, they were here to bust her. She was carrying grass in her purse, and some loud-mouthed prick had rapped about it. But why two of them? Carol tried to tell herself that they could not touch her. She was no longer some dumb black hooker from Harlem that they could push around. Not any more. She was the receptionist for one of the biggest psychoanalysts in the country. But as the two men moved towards her, Carol's panic increased. There was the feral memory of too many years of hiding in stinking, overcrowded tenement apartments while the white Law broke down doors and hauled away a father, or a sister, or a cousin.

But nothing of the turmoil in her mind showed on her face. At first glance the two detectives saw only a young and nubile, tawny-skinned Negress in a smartly tailored beige dress. Her voice was cool and impersonal. 'May I help you?' she asked.

Then Lt Andrew McGreavy, the older detective, spotted the spreading perspiration stain under the armpit of her dress. He automatically filed it away as an interesting piece of information for future use. The doctor's receptionist was up-tight. McGreavy pulled out a wallet with a worn badge pinned onto the cracked imitation leather. 'Lieutenant McGreavy, Nineteenth Precinct.' He indicated his partner. 'Detective Angeli. We're from the Homicide Division.'

Homicide? A muscle in Carol's arm twitched involuntarily. *Chick! He had killed someone. He had broken his promise to her and gone back to the gang. He had pulled a robbery and had shot someone, or – was he shot? Dead? Is that what they had come to tell her?* She felt the perspiration stain begin to widen. Carol suddenly became conscious of it. McGreavy was looking at her face, but she knew that he had noticed it. She and the McGreavys of the world needed no words. They recognized each other on sight. They had known each other for hundreds of years.

'We'd like to see Dr Judd Stevens,' said the younger detective. His voice was gentle and polite, and went with his appearance. She noticed for the first time that he carried a small parcel wrapped in brown paper and held together with string.

It took an instant for his words to sink in. So it wasn't Chick. Or Sammy. Or the grass.

'I'm sorry,' she said, barely hiding her relief. 'Dr Stevens is with a patient.'

'This will only take a few minutes,' McGreavy said. 'We want to ask him some questions.' He paused. 'We can either do it here, or at Police Headquarters.'

She looked at the two of them a moment, puzzled. What the hell could two Homicide detectives want with Dr Stevens? Whatever the police might think, the doctor had not done anything wrong. She knew him too well. How long had it been? Four years. It had started in night court . . .

It was three a.m. and the overhead lights in the courtroom bathed everyone in an unhealthy pallor. The room was old and tired and uncaring, saturated with the stale smell of fear that had accumulated over the years like layers of flaked paint.

It was Carol's lousy luck that Judge Murphy was sitting on the bench again. She had been up before him only two weeks before and had got off with probation. First offence. Meaning it was the first time the bastards had caught her. This time she knew the judge was going to throw the book at her.

The case on the docket ahead of hers was almost over. A tall, quiet-looking man standing before the judge was saying something about his client, a fat man in handcuffs who trembled all over. She figured the quiet-looking man must be a mouthpiece. There was a look about him, an air of easy confidence, that made her feel the fat man was lucky to have him. She didn't have anyone.

The men moved away from the bench and Carol heard her name called. She stood up, pressing her knees together to keep them from trembling. The bailiff gave her a gentle push towards the bench. The court clerk handed the charge sheet to the judge.

Judge Murphy looked at Carol, then at the sheet of paper in front of him.

'"Carol Roberts. Soliciting on the streets, vagrancy, possession of marijuana, and resisting arrest."'

The last was a lot of shit. The policeman had shoved her and she had kicked him in the balls. After all, she was an American citizen.

'You were in here a few weeks ago, weren't you, Carol?'

She made her voice sound uncertain. 'I believe I was, Your Honour.'

'And I gave you probation.'

'Yes, sir.'

'How old are you?'

She should have known they would ask. 'Sixteen. Today's my sixteenth birthday. Happy birthday to me,' she said. And she burst into tears, huge sobs that wracked her body.

The tall, quiet man had been standing at a table at the side gathering up some papers and putting them in a leather attache case. As Carol stood there sobbing, he looked up and watched her for a moment. Then he spoke to Judge Murphy.

The judge called a recess and the two men disappeared into the judge's chambers. Fifteen minutes later, the bailiff escorted Carol into the judge's chambers, where the quiet man was earnestly talking to the judge.

'You're a lucky girl, Carol,' Judge Murphy said. 'You're going to get another chance. The Court is remanding you to the personal custody of Dr Stevens.'

So the tall mother wasn't a mouthpiece – he was a quack. She wouldn't have cared if he was Jack the Ripper. All she wanted was to get out of that stinking courtroom before they found out it wasn't her birthday.

The doctor drove her to his apartment, making small talk that did not require any answers, giving Carol a chance to pull herself together and think things out. He stopped the car in front of a modern apartment building on Seventy-first Street overlooking the East River. The building had a doorman and an elevator operator, and from the calm way they greeted him, you would think he came home every morning at three a.m. with a sixteen-year-old black hooker.

Carol had never seen an apartment like the doctor's. The living-room was done in white with two long, low couches covered in oatmeal tweed. Between the couches was an enormous square coffee table with a thick glass top. On it was a large chessboard with carved Venetian figures. Modern paintings hung on the wall. In the foyer was a closed-circuit television monitor that showed the entrance to the lobby. In one corner of the living-room was a smoked glass bar with shelves of crystal glasses and decanters. Looking out the window, Carol could see tiny boats, far below, tossing their way along the East River.

'Courts always make me hungry,' Judd said. 'Why

don't I whip up a little birthday supper?' And he took her into the kitchen where she watched him skilfully put together a Mexican omelette, French-fried potatoes, toasted English muffins, a salad, and coffee. 'That's one of the advantages of being a bachelor,' he said. 'I can cook when I feel like it.'

So he was a bachelor without any home pussy. If she played her cards right, this could turn out to be a bonanza. When she had finished devouring the meal, he had taken her into the guest bedroom. The bedroom was done in blue, dominated by a large double bed with a blue checked bedspread. There was a low Spanish dresser of dark wood with brass fittings.

'You can spend the night here,' he said. 'I'll rustle up a pair of pyjamas for you.'

As Carol looked around the tastefully decorated room she thought, *Carol, baby! You've hit the jackpot! This mother's looking for a piece of jailbait black ass. And you're the baby who is gonna give it to him.*

She undressed and spent the next half hour in the shower. When she came out, a towel wrapped around her shining, voluptuous body, she saw that the mother-fucking ofay had placed a pair of his pyjamas on the bed. She laughed knowingly and left them there. She threw the towel down and strolled into the living-room. He was not there. She looked through the door leading into a den. He was sitting at a large, comfortable desk with an old-fashioned desk lamp hanging over it. The den was crammed with books from floor to ceiling. She walked up behind him and kissed him on the neck. 'Let's get started, baby,' she whispered. 'You got me so horny I can't stand it.' She pressed closer to him.

'What are we waitin' for, big daddy? If you don't ball me quick, I'll go out of my cotton-pickin' mind.'

He regarded her for a second with thoughtful dark grey eyes. 'Haven't you got enough trouble?' he asked mildly. 'You can't help being born a Negro, but who told you you had to be a black dropout pot-smoking sixteen-year-old whore?'

She stared at him, baffled, wondering what she had said wrong. Maybe he had to get himself worked up and whip her first to get his kicks. Or maybe it was the Reverend Davidson bit. He was going to pray over her black ass, reform her, and then lay her. She tried again. She reached between his legs and stroked him, whispering, 'Go, baby. Sock it to me.'

He gently disengaged himself and sat her in an armchair. She had never been so puzzled. He didn't look like a fag, but these days you never knew. 'What's your bag, baby? Tell me how you like to freak out and I'll give it to you.'

'All right,' he said. 'Let's rap.'

'You mean – *talk*?'

'That's right.'

And they talked. All night long. It was the strangest night that Carol had ever spent. Dr Stevens kept leaping from one subject to another, exploring, testing her. He asked her opinion about Vietnam, ghettos, and college riots. Every time Carol thought she had figured out what he was really after, he switched to another subject. They talked of things she had never heard of, and about subjects in which she considered herself the world's greatest living expert. Months afterwards she used to lie awake, trying to recall the word, the idea, the magic phrase that had changed her. She had never been able to

15

because she finally realized that there had been no magic word. What Dr Stevens had done was simple. He had talked to her. Really talked to her. No one had ever done that before. He had treated her like a human being, an equal, whose opinions and feelings he cared about.

Somewhere during the course of the night she suddenly became aware of her nakedness and went in and put on his pyjamas. He came in and sat on the edge of the bed and they talked some more. They talked about Mao Tse-tung and hula hoops and the Pill. And having a mother and father who had never been married. Carol told him things she had never told anybody in her life. Things that had been long buried deep in her subconscious. And when she had finally fallen asleep, she had felt totally empty. It was as though she had had a major operation, and a river of poison had been drained out of her.

In the morning, after breakfast, he handed her a hundred dollars.

She hesitated, then finally said, 'I lied. It's not my birthday.'

'I know.' He grinned. 'But we won't tell the judge.' His tone changed. 'You can take the money and walk out of here and no one will bother you until the next time you get caught by the police.' He paused. 'I need a receptionist. I think you'd be marvellous at the job.'

She looked at him unbelievingly. 'You're putting me on. I can't take shorthand or type.'

'You could if you went back to school.'

Carol looked at him a moment and then said enthusiastically, 'I never thought of that. That sounds groovy.' She couldn't wait to get the hell out of the apartment with his hundred dollars and flash it at the boys and girls at Fishman's Drug Store in Harlem, where the gang hung out. She could buy enough kicks with this money to last a week.

When she walked into Fishman's Drug Store, it was as though she had never been away. She saw the same bitter faces and heard the same hip, defeated chatter. She was home. She kept thinking of the doctor's apartment. It wasn't the furniture that made the big difference. It was so – clean. And quiet. It was like a little island somewhere in another world. And he had offered her a passport to it. What was there to lose? She could try it for laughs, to show the doctor that he was wrong, that she couldn't make it.

To her own great surprise, Carol enrolled in night school. She left her furnished room with the rust-stained washbasin and broken toilet and the torn green window shade and the lumpy iron cot where she would turn tricks and act out plays. She was a beautiful heiress in Paris or London or Rome, and the man pumping away on top of her was a wealthy, handsome prince, dying to marry her. And as each man had his orgasm and crawled off her, her dream died. Until the next time.

She left the room and all her princes without a backward glance and moved back in with her parents. Dr Stevens gave her an allowance while she was studying. She finished high school with top grades. The doctor was there on graduation day, his grey eyes bright with pride. Someone believed in her. She was somebody. She took a day job at Nedick's and took a secretarial course at night. The day after she finished, she went to work for Dr Stevens and could afford her own apartment.

In the four years that had passed Dr Stevens had always treated her with the same grave courtesy he had shown her the first night. At first she had waited for him to make some reference to what she had been, and what she had become. But she had finally come to the realization that he had always seen her as what she was *now*. All he had done was to help her fulfil herself. Whenever she had a problem, he always found time to discuss it with her. Recently she had been meaning to tell him about what had happened with her and Chick and ask him whether she should tell Chick, but she kept putting it off. She wanted her Dr Stevens to be proud of her. She would have done anything for him. She would have slept with him, killed for him . . .

And now here were these two mothers from the Homicide Squad wanting to see him.

McGreavy was getting impatient. 'How about it, miss?' he asked.

'I have orders never to disturb him when he's with a patient,' said Carol. She saw the expression that came into McGreavy's eyes. 'I'll ring him.' She picked up the phone and pressed the intercom buzzer. After thirty seconds of silence, Dr Stevens' voice came over the phone. 'Yes?'

'There are two detectives here to see you, Doctor. They're from the Homicide Division.'

She listened for a change in his voice . . . nervousness . . . fear. There was nothing. 'They'll have to wait,' he said. He went off the line.

A surge of pride flared through her. Maybe they could panic her, but they could never get her doctor to lose his cool. She looked up defiantly. 'You heard him,' she said.

'How long will his patient be in there?' asked Angeli, the younger man.

She glanced at the clock on the desk. 'Another twenty-five minutes. It's his last patient for the day.'

The two men exchanged a look.

'We'll wait,' sighed McGreavy.

They took chairs. McGreavy was studying her. 'You look familiar,' he said.

She wasn't deceived. The mother was on a fishing expedition. 'You know what they say,' replied Carol. 'We all look alike.'

Exactly twenty-five minutes later, Carol heard the click of the side door that led from the doctor's private office directly to the corridor. A few minutes later, the door of the doctor's office opened and Dr Judd Stevens stepped out. He hesitated as he saw McGreavy. 'We've met before,' he said. He could not remember where.

McGreavy nodded impassively. 'Yeah . . . Lieutenant McGreavy.' He indicated Angeli. 'Detective Frank Angeli.'

Judd and Angeli shook hands. 'Come in.'

The men walked into Judd's private office and the door closed. Carol looked after them, trying to piece it together. The big detective had seemed antagonistic towards Dr Stevens. But maybe that was just his natural charm. Carol was sure of only one thing. Her dress would have to go to the cleaner's.

Judd's office was furnished like a French country living-room. There was no working desk. Instead, comfortable easy chairs and end tables with authentic antique lamps were scattered about the room. At the far end of the office a private door led out to the corridor. On the floor was an exquisitely patterned Edward Fields area rug, and in a corner was a comfortable damask-covered contour couch. McGreavy noted that there were no diplomas on the walls. But he had checked before coming here. If Dr Stevens had wanted to, he could have covered his walls with diplomas and certificates.

'This is the first psychiatrist's office I've ever been in,' Angeli said, openly impressed. 'I wish my house looked like this.'

'It relaxes my patients,' Judd said easily. 'And by the way, I'm a psychoanalyst.'

'Sorry,' Angeli said. 'What's the difference?'

'About fifty dollars an hour,' McGreavy said. 'My partner doesn't get around much.'

Partner. And Judd suddenly remembered. McGreavy's partner had been shot and killed and McGreavy had been wounded during the holdup of a liquor store four – or was it five? – years ago. A petty hoodlum named Amos Ziffren had been arrested for the crime. Ziffren's attorney had pleaded his client not guilty by reason of insanity. Judd had been called in as an expert for the defence and asked to examine Ziffren. He had found that he was hopelessly insane with advanced paresis. On Judd's testimony, Ziffren had escaped the death penalty and had been sent to a mental institution.

'I remember you now,' Judd said. 'The Ziffren case. You had three bullets in you; your partner was killed.'

'And I remember you,' McGreavy said. 'You got the killer off.'

'What can I do for you?'

20

'We need some information, Doctor,' McGreavy said. He nodded to Angeli. Angeli began fumbling at the string on the package he carried.

'We'd like you to identify something for us,' McGreavy said. His voice was careful, giving nothing away.

Angeli had the package open. He held up a yellow oilskin rain slicker. 'Have you ever seen this before?'

'It looks like mine,' Judd said in surprise.

'It is yours. At least your name is stencilled inside.'

'Where did you find it?'

'Where do you think we found it?' The two men were no longer casual. A subtle change had taken place in their faces.

Judd studied McGreavy a moment, then picked up a pipe from a rack on a long, low table and began to fill it with tobacco from a jar. 'I think you'd better tell me what this is all about,' he said quietly.

'It's about this raincoat, Dr Stevens,' said McGreavy. 'If it's yours, we want to know how it got out of your possession.'

'There's no mystery about it. It was drizzling when I came in this morning. My raincoat was at the cleaners, so I wore the yellow slicker. I keep it for fishing trips. One of my patients hadn't brought a raincoat. It was beginning to snow pretty heavily, so I let him borrow the slicker.' He stopped, suddenly worried. 'What's happened to him?'

'Happened to who?' McGreavy asked.

'My patient – John Hanson.'

'Check,' Angeli said gently. 'You hit the bull's-eye. The reason Mr Hanson couldn't return the coat himself is that he's dead.'

21

Judd felt a small shock go through him. 'Dead?'

'Someone stuck a knife in his back,' McGreavy said.

Judd stared at him incredulously. McGreavy took the coat from Angeli and turned it around so that Judd could see the large, ugly slash in the material. The back of the coat was covered with dull, henna-coloured stains. A feeling of nausea swept over Judd.

'Who would want to kill him?'

'We were hoping that you could tell us, Dr Stevens,' said Angeli. 'Who'd know better than his psycho-analyst?'

Judd shook his head helplessly. 'When did it happen?'

McGreavy answered. 'Eleven o'clock this morning. On Lexington Avenue, about a block from your office. A few dozen people must have seen him fall, but they were busy going home to get ready to celebrate the birth of Christ, so they let him lie there bleeding to death in the snow.'

Judd squeezed the edge of the table, his knuckles white.

'What time was Hanson here this morning?' asked Angeli.

'Ten o'clock.'

'How long do your sessions last, Doctor?'

'Fifty minutes.'

'Did he leave as soon as it was over?'

'Yes. I had another patient waiting.'

'Did Hanson go out through the reception office?'

'No. My patients come in through the reception office and leave by that door.' He indicated the private door leading to the outside corridor. 'In that way they don't meet each other.'

22

McGreavy nodded. 'So Hanson was killed within a few minutes of the time he left here. Why was he coming to see you?'

Judd hesitated. 'I'm sorry. I can't discuss a doctor-patient relationship.'

'Someone murdered him,' McGreavy said. 'You might be able to help us find his killer.'

Judd's pipe had gone out. He took his time lighting it again.

'How long had he been coming to you?' This time it was Angeli. Police teamwork.

'Three years,' Judd said.

'What was his problem?'

Judd hesitated. He saw John Hanson as he had looked that morning; excited, smiling, eager to enjoy his new freedom. 'He was a homosexual.'

'This is going to be another one of those beauties,' McGreavy said bitterly.

'*Was* a homosexual,' Judd said. 'Hanson was cured. I told him this morning that he didn't have to see me any more. He was ready to move back in with his family. He has – had – a wife and two children.'

'A fag with a family?' asked McGreavy.

'It happens often.'

'Maybe one of his homo playmates didn't want to cut him loose. They got in a fight. He lost his temper and slipped a knife in his boyfriend's back.'

Judd considered. 'It's possible,' he said thoughtfully, 'but I don't believe it.'

'Why not, Dr Stevens?' asked Angeli.

'Because Hanson hadn't had any homosexual contacts in more than a year. I think it's much more likely

23

that someone tried to mug him. Hanson was the kind of man who would have put up a fight.'

'A brave married fag,' McGreavy said heavily. He took out a cigar and lit it. 'There's only one thing wrong with the mugger theory. His wallet hadn't been touched. There was over a hundred dollars in it.' He watched Judd's reaction.

Angeli said, 'If we're looking for a nut, it might make it easier.'

'Not necessarily,' Judd objected. He walked over to the window. 'Take a look at that crowd down there. One out of twenty is, has been, or will be in a mental hospital.'

'But if a man's crazy . . . ?'

'He doesn't have to necessarily appear crazy,' Judd explained. 'For every obvious case of insanity there are at least ten cases undiagnosed.'

McGreavy was studying Judd with open interest. 'You know a lot about human nature, don't you, Doctor?'

'There's no such thing as human nature,' Judd said. 'Any more than there's such a thing as animal nature. Try to average out a rabbit and a tiger. Or a squirrel and an elephant.'

'How long you been practising psychoanalysis?' asked McGreavy.

'Twelve years. Why?'

McGreavy shrugged. 'You're a good-looking guy. I'll bet a lot of your patients fall in love with you, huh?'

Judd's eyes chilled. 'I don't understand the point of the question.'

'Oh, come on, Doc. Sure you do. We're both men of

the world. A fag walks in here and finds himself a handsome young doctor to tell his troubles to.' His tone grew confidential. 'Now do you mean to say that in three years on your couch Hanson didn't get a little hard-on for you?'

Judd looked at him without expression. 'Is that your idea of being a man of the world, Lieutenant?'

McGreavy was unperturbed. 'It could have happened. And I'll tell you what else could have happened. You said you told Hanson you didn't want to see him again. Maybe he didn't like that. He'd grown dependent on you in three years. The two of you had a fight.'

Judd's face darkened with anger.

Angeli broke the tension. 'Can you think of anyone who had reason to hate him, Doctor? Or someone *he* might have hated?'

'If there were such a person,' Judd said, 'I would tell you. I think I knew everything there was to know about John Hanson. He was a happy man. He didn't hate anyone and I don't know of anyone who hated him.'

'Good for him. You must be one helluva doctor,' McGreavy said. 'We'll take his file along with us.'

'No.'

'We can get a court order.'

'Get it. There's nothing in that file that can help you.'

'Then what harm could it do if you gave it to us?' asked Angeli.

'It could hurt Hanson's wife and children. You're on the wrong track. You'll find that Hanson was killed by a stranger.'

'I don't believe it,' McGreavy snapped.

Angeli rewrapped the raincoat and tied the string

around the bundle. 'We'll get this back to you when we run some more tests on it.'

'Keep it,' Judd said.

McGreavy opened the private door leading to the corridor. 'We'll be in touch with you, Doctor.' He walked out. Angeli nodded to Judd and followed McGreavy out.

Judd was still standing there, his mind churning, when Carol walked in. 'Is everything all right?' she asked hesitantly.

'Someone killed John Hanson.'

'*Killed* him?'

'He was stabbed,' Judd said.

'Oh my God! But why?'

'The police don't know.'

'How terrible!' She saw his eyes and the pain in them. 'Is there anything I can do, Doctor?'

'Would you close up the office, Carol? I'm going over to see Mrs Hanson. I'd like to break the news to her myself.'

'Don't worry. I'll take care of everything,' said Carol.

'Thanks.'

And Judd left.

Thirty minutes later Carol had finished putting the files away and was locking her desk when the corridor door opened. It was after six o'clock and the building was closed. Carol looked up as the man smiled and moved towards her.

Chapter Three

Mary Hanson was a doll of a woman; small, beautiful, exquisitely made. On the outside, she was soft, Southern-helpless-feminine, and on the inside, granite bitch. Judd had met her a week after beginning her husband's therapy. She had fought hysterically against it and Judd had asked her to have a talk with him. 'Why are you so opposed to your husband going through analysis?'

'I won't have my friends saying I married a crazy man,' she had told Judd. 'Tell him to give me a divorce; then he can do any damn thing he pleases.'

Judd had explained that a divorce at that point could destroy John completely.

'There's nothing left to destroy,' Mary had screamed. 'If I'd known he was a fairy, do you think I would have married him? He's a woman.'

'There's some woman in every man,' Judd had said. 'Just as there's some man in every woman. And in your husband's case, there are some difficult psychological problems to overcome. But he's trying, Mrs Hanson. I think you owe it to him and his children to help him.'

He had reasoned with her for more than three hours, and in the end she had reluctantly agreed to hold off on the divorce. In the months that followed, she had become interested and then involved in the battle that

John was waging. Judd made it a rule never to treat married couples, but Mary had asked him to let her become a patient, and he had found it helpful. As she had begun to understand herself and where she had failed as a wife, John's progress had become dramatically rapid.

And now Judd was here to tell her that her husband had been senselessly murdered. She looked up at him, unable to believe what he had just said, sure that it was some kind of macabre joke. And then realization set in. 'He's never coming back to me!' she screamed. 'He's never coming back to me!' She started tearing at her clothes in anguish, like a wounded animal. The six-year-old twins walked in. And from that moment on, there was bedlam. Judd managed to calm the children down and take them to a neighbour's house. He gave Mrs Hanson a sedative and called the family doctor. When he was sure there was nothing more he could do, he left. He got into his car and drove aimlessly, lost in thought. Hanson had fought his way through a hell, and at the moment of his victory . . . It was such a pointless death. *Could* it have been some homosexual who had attacked him? Some former lover who was frustrated because Hanson had left him? It was possible, of course, but Judd did not believe it. Lieutenant McGreavy had said that Hanson was killed a block away from the office. If the murderer had been a homosexual, full of hatred, he would have made a rendezvous with Hanson at some private place, either to try to persuade Hanson to come back to him or to pour out his recriminations before he killed him. He would not have plunged a knife into him on a crowded street and then fled.

On the corner ahead he saw a phone booth and suddenly remembered that he had promised to have dinner with Dr Peter Hadley and his wife, Norah. They were his closest friends, but he was in no mood to see anyone. He stopped the car at the kerb, went into the phone booth and dialled the Hadleys' number. Norah answered the phone. 'You're late! Where are you?'

'Norah,' Judd said, 'I'm afraid I'm going to have to beg off tonight.'

'You can't,' she wailed. 'I have a sexy blonde sitting here dying to meet you.'

'We'll do it another night,' Judd said. 'I'm really not up to it. Please apologize for me.'

'Doctors!' snorted Norah. 'Just a minute and I'll put your chum on.'

Peter got on the phone. 'Anything wrong, Judd?'

Judd hesitated. 'Just a hard day, Pete. I'll tell you about it tomorrow.'

'You're missing some delicious Scandinavian smorgasbord. I mean *beautiful.*'

'I'll meet her another time,' promised Judd. He heard a hurried whisper, and then Norah got on the phone again.

'She'll be here for Christmas dinner, Judd. Will you come?'

He hesitated. 'We'll talk about it later, Norah. I'm sorry about tonight.' He hung up. He wished he knew of some tactful way to stop Norah's matchmaking.

Judd had got married in his senior years in college. Elizabeth had been a social science major, warm and bright and gay, and they had both been young and very much in love and full of wonderful plans to remake the world for all the children they were going to have. And on the first Christmas of their marriage, Elizabeth and their unborn child had been killed in a head-on automobile collision. Judd had plunged himself totally into his work, and in time had become one of the outstanding psychoanalysts in the country. But he was still not able to bear being with other people celebrating Christmas Day. Somehow, even though he told himself he was wrong, that belonged to Elizabeth and their child.

He pushed open the door of the phone booth. He was aware of a girl standing outside the booth waiting to use the phone. She was young and pretty, dressed in a tight-fitting sweater and a miniskirt, with a bright-coloured raincoat. He stepped out of the booth. 'Sorry,' he apologized.

She gave him a warm smile. 'That's all right.' There was a wistful look on her face. He had seen that look before. Loneliness seeking to break through the barrier that he had unconsciously set up.

If Judd knew that he had a quality that was attractive to women, it was deep in his subconscious. He had never analysed why. It was more of a handicap than an asset to have his female patients falling in love with him. It sometimes made life very difficult.

He moved past the girl with a friendly nod. He sensed her standing there in the rain, watching as he got into his car and drove away.

He turned the car onto the East River Drive and headed for the Merritt Parkway. An hour and a half later he was on the Connecticut Turnpike. The snow in New York was dirty and slushy, but the same storm had magically transformed the Connecticut landscape into a Currier and Ives picture postcard.

He drove past Westport and Danbury, deliberately forcing his mind to concentrate on the ribbon of road that flashed beneath his wheels and the wintry wonderland that surrounded him. Each time his thought reached out to John Hanson, he made himself think of other things. He drove on through the darkness of the Connecticut countryside and hours later, emotionally worn out, finally turned the car around and headed for home.

Mike, the red-faced doorman who usually greeted him with a smile, was preoccupied and distant. Family difficulties, Judd supposed. Usually Judd would chat with him about Mike's teenage son and married daughters, but Judd did not feel like talking this evening. He asked Mike to have the car sent down to the garage.

'Right, Dr Stevens.' Mike seemed about to add something, then thought better of it.

Judd walked into the building. Ben Katz, the manager was crossing the lobby. He saw Judd, gave a nervous wave, and hurriedly disappeared into his apartment.

What's the matter with everyone tonight? thought Judd. *Or is it just my nerves?* He stepped into the elevator.

Eddie, the elevator operator, nodded. 'Evening, Dr Stevens.'

'Good evening, Eddie.'

Eddie swallowed and looked away self-consciously.

'Is anything wrong?' Judd asked.

Eddie quickly shook his head and kept his eyes averted.

My God, thought Judd. *Another candidate for*

my couch. The building was suddenly full of them.

Eddie opened the elevator door and Judd got out. He started towards his apartment. He didn't hear the elevator door close, so he turned around. Eddie was staring at him. As Judd started to speak, Eddie quickly closed the elevator door. Judd went to his apartment, unlocked the door, and entered.

Every light in the apartment was on. Lieutenant McGreavy was opening a drawer in the living-room. Angeli was coming out of the bedroom. Judd felt anger flare in him. 'What are you doing in my apartment?'

'Waitin' for you, Dr Stevens,' McGreavy said.

Judd walked over and slammed the drawer shut, narrowly missing McGreavy's fingers. 'How did you get in here?'

'We have a search warrant,' said Angeli.

Judd stared at him incredulously. 'A search warrant? For my apartment?'

'Suppose we ask the questions, Doctor,' McGreavy said.

'You don't have to answer them,' interjected Angeli, 'without benefit of legal counsel. Also, you should know that anything you say can be used as evidence against you.'

'Do you want to call a lawyer?' McGreavy asked.

'I don't need a lawyer. I told you that I loaned the raincoat to John Hanson this morning and I didn't see it again until you brought it to my office this afternoon. I couldn't have killed him. I was with patients all day. Miss Roberts can verify that.'

McGreavy and Angeli exchanged a silent signal.

'Where did you go after you left your office this afternoon?' Angeli said.

'To see Mrs Hanson.'

'We know that,' McGreavy said. 'Afterwards.'

Judd hesitated. 'I drove around.'

'Where?'

'I drove up to Connecticut.'

'Where did you stop for dinner?' McGreavy asked.

'I didn't. I wasn't hungry.'

'So no one saw you?'

Judd thought for a moment. 'I suppose not.'

'Perhaps you stopped for gas somewhere,' suggested Angeli.

'No,' Judd said. 'I didn't. What difference does it make where I went tonight? Hanson was killed this morning.'

'Did you go back to your office any time after you left it this afternoon?' McGreavy's voice was casual.

'No,' Judd said. 'Why?'

'It was broken into.'

'What? By whom?'

'We don't know,' said McGreavy. 'I want you to come down and take a look around. You can tell us if anything is missing.'

'Of course,' Judd replied. 'Who reported it?'

'The night watchman,' said Angeli. 'Do you keep anything of value in the office, Doctor? Cash? Drugs? Anything like that?'

'Petty cash,' Judd said. 'No addictive drugs. There was nothing there to steal. It doesn't make any sense.'

'Right,' McGreavy said. 'Let's go.'

In the elevator Eddie gave Judd an apologetic look. Judd met his eyes and nodded that he understood.

Surely, Judd thought, the police couldn't suspect him

33

of breaking into his own office. It was as though McGreavy was determined to pin something on him because of his dead partner. But that had been five years ago. Could McGreavy have been brooding all these years, blaming it on the doctor? Waiting for a chance to get him?

There was an unmarked police car a few feet from the entrance. They got in and rode to the office in silence.

When they reached the office building, Judd signed the lobby register. Bigelow, the guard, looked at him strangely. Or did he imagine it?

They took the elevator to the fifteenth floor and walked down the corridor to Judd's office. A uniformed policeman was standing in front of the door. He nodded to McGreavy and stepped aside. Judd reached for his key.

'The door's unlocked,' Angeli said. He pushed the door open and they went in, Judd leading the way.

The reception office was in chaos. All the drawers had been pulled out of the desk and papers were strewn about the floor. Judd stared unbelievingly, feeling a shock of personal violation.

'What do you suppose they were looking for, Doctor?' asked McGreavy.

'I have no idea,' Judd said. He walked to the inner door and opened it, McGreavy close behind him.

In his office two end tables had been overturned, a smashed lamp lay on the floor, and blood soaked the Fields rug.

In the far corner of the room, grotesquely spread out, was the body of Carol Roberts. She was nude. Her hands were tied behind her back with piano wire, and acid had been splashed on her face and breasts and between her thighs. The fingers of her right hand were broken. Her face was battered and swollen. A wadded handkerchief was stuffed in her mouth.

The two detectives watched Judd as he stared at the body.

'You look pale,' Angeli said. 'Sit down.'

Judd shook his head and took several deep breaths. When he spoke, his voice was shaking with rage. 'Who – who could have done this?'

'That's what you're going to tell us, Dr Stevens,' said McGreavy.

Judd looked up at him. 'No one could have wanted to do this to Carol. She never hurt anyone in her life.'

'I think it's about time you started singing another tune.' McGreavy said. 'No one wanted to hurt Hanson, but they stuck a knife in his back. No one wanted to hurt Carol, but they poured acid all over her and tortured her to death.' His voice became hard. 'And you stand there and tell me no one would want to hurt them. What the hell are you – deaf, dumb, and blind? The girl worked for you for four years. You're a psychoanalyst. Are you trying to tell me you didn't know or care about her personal life?'

'Of course I cared,' Judd said tightly. 'She had a boyfriend she was going to marry – '

'Chick. We've talked to him.'

'But he could never have done this. He's a decent boy and he loved Carol.'

'When was the last time you saw Carol alive?' asked Angeli.

'I told you. When I left here to go to see Mrs

Hanson. I asked Carol to close up the office.' His voice broke and he swallowed and took a deep breath.

'Were you scheduled to see any more patients today?'

'No.'

'Do you think this could have been done by a maniac?' Angeli asked.

'It must have been a maniac, but – even a maniac has to have some motivation.'

'That's what I think,' McGreavy said.

Judd looked over to where Carol's body lay. It had the sad appearance of a disfigured rag doll, useless and discarded. 'How long are you going to leave her like this?' Judd asked angrily.

'They'll take her away now,' said Angeli. 'The coroner and the Homicide boys have already finished.'

Judd turned to McGreavy. 'You left her like this for me?'

'Yeah,' McGreavy said. 'I'm going to ask you again. Is there anything in this office that someone could want badly enough to' – he indicated Carol – 'do that?'

'No.'

'What about the records of your patients?'

Judd shook his head. 'Nothing.'

'You're not being very cooperative, Doctor, are you?' asked McGreavy.

'Don't you think I want to see you find whoever did this?' Judd snapped. 'If there was anything in my files that would help, I would tell you. I know my patients. There isn't any one among them who could have killed her. This was done by an outsider.'

'How do you know it wasn't someone after your files?'

'My files weren't touched.'

McGreavy looked at him with quickened interest. 'How do you know that?' he asked. 'You haven't even looked.'

Judd walked over to the far wall. As the two men watched, he pressed the lower section of the panelling and the wall slid open, revealing racks of built-in shelves. They were filled with tapes. 'I record every session with my patients,' Judd said. 'I keep the tapes here.'

'Couldn't they have tortured Carol to try to force her to tell where those tapes were?'

'There is nothing in any of these tapes worth anything to anyone. There was some other motive for her murder.'

Judd looked at Carol's scarred body again, and he was filled with helpless, blind rage. 'You've got to find whoever did this!'

'I intend to,' McGreavy said. He was looking at Judd.

On the windy, deserted street in front of Judd's office building, McGreavy told Angeli to drive Judd home. 'I've got an errand to do,' McGreavy said. He turned to Judd. 'Goodnight, Doctor.'

Judd watched the huge, lumbering figure move down the street.

'Let's go,' Angeli said. 'I'm freezing.'

Judd slid into the front seat beside Angeli, and the car pulled away from the kerb.

'I've got to go tell Carol's family,' Judd said.

'We've already been over there.'

Judd nodded wearily. He still wanted to see them himself, but it could wait.

37

There was a silence. Judd wondered what errand Lieutenant McGreavy could have at this hour of the morning.

As though reading his thoughts, Angeli said, 'McGreavy's a good cop. He thought Ziffren should have got the electric chair for killing his partner.'

'Ziffren was insane.'

Angeli shrugged. 'I'll take your word for it, Doctor.'

But McGreavy hadn't, Judd thought. He turned his mind to Carol and remembered her brightness and her affection and her deep pride in what she was doing, and Angeli was speaking to him and he saw that they had arrived at his apartment building.

Five minutes later Judd was in his apartment. There was no question of sleep. He fixed himself a brandy and carried it into his den. He remembered the night Carol had strolled in here, naked and beautiful, rubbing her warm, lithe body against his. He had acted cool and aloof because he had known that that was the only chance he had of helping her. But she had never known what willpower it had taken for him to keep from making love to her. Or had she? He raised his brandy glass and drained it.

The city morgue looked like all city morgues at three o'clock in the morning, except that someone had placed a wreath of mistletoe over the door. Someone, thought McGreavy, who had either an overabundance of holiday spirit or a macabre sense of humour.

McGreavy had waited impatiently in the corridor until the autopsy was completed. When the coroner waved to him, he walked into the sickly-white autopsy room. The coroner was scrubbing his hands at the large

38

white sink. He was a small, birdlike man with a high, chirping voice and quick, nervous movements. He answered all of McGreavy's questions in a rapid, staccato manner, then fled. McGreavy remained there a few minutes, absorbed in what he had just learned. Then he walked out into the freezing night air to find a taxi. There was no sign of one. The sons of bitches were all vacationing in Bermuda. He could stand out here until his ass froze off. He spotted a police cruiser, flagged it down, showed his identification to the young rookie behind the wheel, and ordered him to drive him to the Nineteenth Precinct. It was against regulations, but what the hell. It was going to be a long night.

When McGreavy walked into the precinct, Angeli was waiting for him. 'They just finished the autopsy on Carol Roberts,' McGreavy said.

'And?'

'She was pregnant.'

Angeli looked at him in surprise.

'She was three months gone. A little late to have a safe abortion, and a little early to show.'

'Do you think that had anything to do with her murder?'

'That's a good question,' McGreavy said. 'If Carol's boyfriend knocked her up and they were going to get married anyway – what's the big deal? So they get married and have the kid a few months later. It happens every day of the week. On the other hand, if he knocked her up and he *didn't* want to marry her – that's no big deal, either. So she has the baby and no husband. That happens *twice* every day of the week.'

'We talked to Chick. He wanted to marry her.'

'I know,' replied McGreavy. 'So we have to ask ourselves where that leaves us. It leaves us with a coloured girl who's pregnant. She goes to the father and tells him about it, and he murders her.'

'He'd have to be insane.'

'Or very foxy. Look at it this way: supposing Carol went to the father and broke the bad news and told him she wasn't going to have an abortion; she was going to have his baby. Maybe she used it to try to blackmail him into marrying her. But supposing he couldn't marry her because he was married already. Or maybe he was a white man. Let's say a well-known doctor with a fancy practice. If a thing like this ever got out, it would ruin him. Who the hell would go to a head-shrinker who knocked up his coloured receptionist and had to marry her?'

'Stevens is a doctor,' said Angeli. 'There are a dozen ways he could have killed her without arousing suspicion.'

'Maybe,' McGreavy said. 'Maybe not. If there was any suspicion and it could be traced back to him, he'd have a hard time getting out of it. He buys poison – someone has a record of it. He buys a rope or a knife – they can all be traced. But look at this cute little setup. Some maniac comes in for no reason and murders his receptionist and he's the grief-stricken employer demanding that the police find the killer.'

'It sounds like a pretty flimsy case.'

'I'm not finished. Let's take his patient, John Hanson. Another senseless killing by this unknown maniac. I'll tell you something, Angeli. I don't believe in coincidences. And two coincidences like that in one day make me nervous. So I asked myself what connection there could be between the death of John Hanson and Carol Roberts, and suddenly it didn't seem so coincidental, after all. Suppose Carol walked into his office and broke the bad news that he was going to be a daddy. They had a big fight and she tried to blackmail him. She said he had to marry her, give her money – whatever. John Hanson was waiting in the outer office, listening. Maybe Stevens wasn't sure he had heard anything until he got on the couch. Then Hanson threatened him with exposure. Or tried to get him to sleep with him.'

'That's a lot of guesswork.'

'But it fits. When Hanson left, the doctor slipped out and fixed him so he couldn't talk. Then he had to come back and get rid of Carol. He made it look like some maniac did the job, then he stopped by to see Mrs Hanson, and took a ride to Connecticut. Now his problems are solved. He's sitting pretty and the police are running their asses off searching for some unknown nut.'

'I can't buy it,' Angeli said. 'You're trying to build a murder case without a shred of concrete evidence.'

'What do you call "concrete"?' McGreavy asked. 'We've got two corpses. One of them is a pregnant lady who worked for Stevens. The other is one of his patients, murdered a block from his office. He's coming to him for treatment because he's a homosexual. When I asked to listen to his tapes, he wouldn't let me. Why? Who is Dr Stevens protecting? I asked him if anyone could have broken into his office looking for something. Then maybe we could have cooked up a nice theory that Carol caught them and they tortured her to

41

try to find out where this mysterious something was. But guess what? There is no mysterious something. His tapes aren't worth a tinker's damn to anybody. He had no drugs in the office. No money. So we're looking for some goddamn maniac. Right? Except that I won't buy it. I think we're looking for Dr Judd Stevens.'

'I think you're out to nail him,' said Angeli quietly.

McGreavy's face flushed with anger. 'Because he's as guilty as hell.'

'Are you going to arrest him?'

'I'm going to give Dr Stevens some rope,' McGreavy said. 'And while he's hanging himself, I'm going to be digging into every little skeleton in his closet. When I nail him, he's going to stay nailed.' McGreavy turned and walked out.

Angeli looked after him thoughtfully. If he did nothing, there was a good chance that McGreavy would try to railroad Dr Stevens. He could not let that happen. He made a mental note to speak to Captain Bertelli in the morning.

Chapter Four

The morning newspapers headlined the sensational torture murder of Carol Roberts. Judd was tempted to have his telephone exchange call his patients and cancel his appointments for the day. He had not gone to bed, and his eyes felt heavy and gritty. But when he reviewed the list of patients, he decided that two of them would be desperate if he cancelled; three of them would be badly upset; the others could be handled. He decided it was better to continue with his normal routine, partly for his patients' sake, and partly because it was good therapy for him to try to keep his mind off what had happened.

Judd arrived at his office early, but already the corridor was crowded with newspaper and television reporters and photographers. He refused to let them in or to make a statement, and finally managed to get rid of them. He opened the door to his inner office slowly, filled with trepidation. But the blood-stained rug had been removed and everything else had been put back in place. The office looked normal. Except that Carol would never walk in here again, smiling and full of life.

Judd heard the outer door open. His first patient had arrived.

Harrison Burke was a distinguished-looking silver-haired man who looked like the prototype of a big business executive, which he was: a vice-president of the International Steel Corporation. When Judd had first seen Burke, he had wondered whether the executive had created his stereotyped image, or whether the image had created the executive. Some day he would write a book on face values; a doctor's bedside manner, a lawyer's flamboyance in a court-room, an actress's face and figure – these were the universal currencies of acceptance: the surface image rather than the basic values.

Burke lay down on the couch, and Judd turned his attention to him. Burke had been sent to Judd by Dr Peter Hadley two months ago. It had taken Judd ten minutes to ascertain that Harrison Burke was a paranoiac with tendencies towards homicide. The morning headlines had been full of a murder that had taken place in this office the night before, but Burke never mentioned it. That was typical of his condition. He was totally immersed in himself.

'You didn't believe me before,' Burke said, 'but now I've got proof that they're after me.'

'I thought we had decided to keep an open mind about that, Harrison,' Judd replied carefully. 'Remember yesterday we agreed that the imagination could play – '

'It isn't my imagination,' shouted Burke. He sat up, his fists clenched. 'They're trying to kill me!'

'Why don't you lie down and try to relax?' Judd suggested soothingly.

Burke got to his feet. 'Is that all you've got to say? You don't even want to hear my proof!' His eyes narrowed. 'How do I know you're not one of them?'

'You know I'm not one of them,' Judd said. 'I'm your

friend. I'm trying to help you.' He felt a stab of disappointment. The progress he had thought they were making over the past month had completely eroded away. He was looking now at the same terrified paranoiac who had first walked into his office two months ago.

Burke had started with International Steel as a mail boy. In twenty-five years his distinguished good looks and his affable personality had taken him almost to the top of the corporate ladder. He had been next in line for the presidency. Then, four years ago, his wife and three children had perished in a fire at their summer home in Southampton. Burke had been in the Bahamas with his mistress. He had taken the tragedy harder than anyone realized. Reared as a devout Catholic, he was unable to shake off his burden of guilt. He began to brood, and he saw less of his friends. He stayed home evenings, reliving the agonies of his wife and children burning to death while, in another part of his mind, he lay in bed with his mistress. It was like a motion picture that he ran over and over in his mind. He blamed himself completely for the death of his family. If only he had been there, he could have saved them. The thought became an obsession. He was a monster. He knew it and God knew it. Surely others could see it! They must hate him as he hated himself. People smiled at him and pretended sympathy, but all the while they were waiting for him to expose himself, waiting to trap him. But he was too cunning for them. He stopped going to the executive dining-room and began to have lunch in the privacy of his office. He avoided everyone as much as possible.

Two years ago, when the company had needed a new

president, they had passed over Harrison Burke and had hired an outsider. A year later the post of executive vice-president had opened up, and a man was given the job over Burke's head. Now he had all the proof he needed that there was a conspiracy against him. He began to spy on the people around him. At night he hid tape recorders in the offices of other executives. Six months ago he had been caught. It was only because of his long seniority and position that he was not fired.

Trying to help him and relieve some of the pressure on him, the president of the company began to cut down on Burke's responsibilities. Instead of helping, it convinced Burke more than ever that *they* were out to get him. *They* were afraid of him because he was smarter than they were. If he became president, *they* would all lost their jobs because *they* were stupid fools. He began to make more and more mistakes. When these errors were called to his attention, he indignantly denied having made them. Someone was deliberately changing his reports, altering the figures and statistics, trying to discredit him. Soon he realized that it was not only the people in the company who were after him. There were spies outside. He was constantly followed in the streets. They tapped his telephone line, read his mail. He was afraid to eat, lest they poison his food. His weight began to drop alarmingly. The worried president of the company arranged an appointment for him with Dr Peter Hadley and insisted that Burke keep it. After spending half an hour with him, Dr Hadley had phoned Judd. Judd's appointment book was full, but when Peter had told him how urgent it was, Judd reluctantly agreed to take him on.

Now Harrison Burke lay supine on the damask-covered contour couch, his fists clenched tightly at his sides.

'Tell me about your proof.'

'They broke into my house last night. They came to kill me. But I was too clever for them. I sleep in my den now and I have extra locks on all the doors so they can't get to me.'

'Did you report the break-in to the police?' Judd asked.

'Of course not! The police are in it with them. They have orders to shoot me. But they wouldn't dare do it while there are other people around, so I stay in crowds.'

'I'm glad you gave me this information,' Judd said.

'What are you going to do with it?' Burke asked eagerly.

'I'm listening very carefully to everything you say,' Judd said. He indicated the tape recorder. 'I've got it all down on tape so if they do kill you, we'll have a record of the conspiracy.'

Burke's face lit up. 'By God, that's good! Tape! That'll really fix them!'

'Why don't you lie down again?' Judd suggested.

Burke nodded and slid onto the couch. He closed his eyes. 'I'm tired. I haven't slept in months. I don't dare close my eyes. You don't know what it's like, having everybody after you.'

Don't I? He thought of McGreavy.

'Didn't your houseboy hear anyone break in?' Judd asked.

'Didn't I tell you?' Burke replied. 'I fired him two weeks ago.'

47

Judd quickly went over in his mind his recent sessions with Harrison Burke. Only three days ago Burke had described a fight he had had that day with his houseboy. So his sense of time had become disoriented. 'I don't believe you mentioned it,' Judd said casually. 'Are you sure it was two weeks ago that you let him go?'

'I don't make mistakes,' snapped Burke. 'How the hell do you think I got to be vice-president of one of the biggest corporations in the world? Because I've got a brilliant mind, Doctor, and don't forget it.'

'Why did you fire him?'

'He tried to poison me.'

'How?'

'With a plate of ham and eggs. Loaded with arsenic.'

'Did you taste it?' Judd asked.

'Of course not,' Burke snorted.

'How did you know it was poisoned?'

'I could smell the poison.'

'What did you say to him?'

A look of satisfaction came over Burke's face. 'I didn't say anything. I beat the shit out of him.'

A feeling of frustration swept over Judd. Given time, he was sure he could have helped Harrison Burke. But time had run out. There was always the danger in psychoanalysis that under the venting of free-flow association, the thin veneer of the id could blow wide open, letting escape all the primitive passions and emotions that huddled together in the mind like terrified wild beasts in the night. The free verbalizing was the first step in treatment. In Burke's case, it had boomeranged. These sessions had released all the latent hostilities that had been locked in his mind.

Burke had seemed to improve with each session, agreeing with Judd that there was no conspiracy, that he was only over-worked and emotionally exhausted. Judd had felt that he was guiding Burke to a point where they could begin deep analysis and start to attack the root of the problem. But Burke had been cunningly lying all along. He had been testing Judd, leading him on to try to trap him and find out whether he was one of *them*. Harrison Burke was a walking time bomb that could explode at any second. There was no next of kin to notify. Should Judd call the president of the company and tell him what he felt? If he did, it would instantly destroy Burke's future. He would have to be put away in an institution. Was he right in his diagnosis that Burke was a potential homicidal paranoiac? He would like to get another opinion before he called, but Burke would never consent. Judd knew he would have to make the decision alone.

'Harrison, I want you to make me a promise,' Judd said.

'What kind of promise?' Burke asked warily.

'If they are trying to trick you, then they want you to do something violent so they can have you locked up . . . But you're too smart for that. No matter how they provoke you, I want you to promise me that you won't do anything to them. That way, they can't touch you.'

Burke's eyes lit up. 'By God, you're right,' he said. 'So that's their plan! Well, we're too clever for them, aren't we?'

Outside, Judd heard the sound of the reception door open and close. He looked at his watch. His next patient was here.

Judd quietly snapped off the tape recorder. 'I think that's enough for today,' he said.

'You got all this down on the tape recorder?' Burke asked eagerly.

'Every word,' Judd said. 'No one's going to hurt you.' He hesitated. 'I don't think you should go to the office today. Why don't you go home and get some rest?'

'I can't,' Burke whispered, his voice filled with despair. 'If I'm not in my office, they'll take my name off the door and put someone else's name on it.' He leaned towards Judd. 'Be careful. If they know you're my friend, they'll try to get you, too.' Burke walked over to the door leading to the corridor. He opened it a crack and peered up and down the corridor. Then he swiftly sidled out.

Judd looked after him, his mind filled with the pain of what he would have to do to Harrison Burke's life. Perhaps if Burke had come to him six months earlier . . . And then a sudden thought sent a chill through him. Was Harrison Burke *already* a murderer? Was it possible that he had been involved in the deaths of John Hanson and Carol Roberts? Both Burke and Hanson were patients. And they could have easily met. Several times in the past few months Burke's appointments had followed Hanson's. And Burke had been late more than once. He could have run into Hanson in the corridor. And seeing him several times could easily have triggered his paranoia, made him feel that Hanson was following him, threatening him. As for Carol, Burke had seen her every time he came to the office. Had his sick mind conceived some menace from her that could only be removed by her death? How long had Burke really been mentally ill? His wife and three children had died in an accidental fire. Accidental? Somehow, he had to find out.

He went to the door leading to the reception office and opened it. 'Come in,' he said.

Anne Blake rose gracefully to her feet and moved towards him, a warm smile lighting her face. Judd felt again the same heart-turning feeling that had hit him when he had first seen her. It was the first time that he had felt any deep emotional response towards any woman since Elizabeth.

In no way did they look alike. Elizabeth had been blonde and small and blue-eyed. Anne Blake had black hair and unbelievable violet eyes framed by long, dark lashes. She was tall, with a lovely, full-curved figure. She had an air of lively intelligence and a classical patrician beauty that would have made her seem inaccessible, except for the warmth in her eyes. Her voice was low and soft, with a faint, husky quality.

Anne was in her middle twenties. She was, without question, the most beautiful woman Judd had ever seen. But it was something beyond her beauty that caught at Judd. There was an almost palpable force that pulled him to her, some unexplainable reaction that made him feel as though emotions long since dead had suddenly surfaced again, surprising him by their intensity.

She had appeared in Judd's office three weeks earlier, without an appointment. Carol had explained that his schedule was full and he could not possibly take on any new patients. But Anne had quietly asked if she could wait. She had sat in the outer office for two hours, and Carol had finally taken pity on her and brought her in to Judd.

He had felt such an instant powerful emotional reaction to Anne that he had no idea what she said during the first few minutes. He remembered he had asked her to sit down and she had told him her name, Anne Blake. She was a housewife. Judd had asked her what her problem was. She had hesitated and said that she was not certain. She was not even sure she had a problem. A doctor friend of hers had mentioned that Judd was one of the most brilliant analysts in the country, but when Judd had asked who the doctor was, Anne had demurred. For all Judd knew, she could have got his name out of the telephone directory.

He had tried to explain to her how impossible his schedule was, that he simply was unable to take on any new patients. He offered to recommend half a dozen good analysts. But Anne had quietly insisted that she wanted him to treat her. In the end Judd had agreed. Outwardly, except for the fact that she appeared to be under some stress, she seemed perfectly normal, and he was certain that her problem would be a relatively simple one, easily solved. He broke his rule about not taking any patient without another doctor's recommendation, and he gave up his lunch hour in order to treat Anne. She had appeared twice a week for the past three weeks, and Judd knew very little more about her than he had known when she first came in. He knew something more about himself: He was in love – for the first time since Elizabeth.

At their first session, Judd had asked her if she loved her husband, and hated himself for wanting to hear her say that she did not. But she had said, 'Yes. He's a kind man, and very strong.'

'Do you think he represents a father figure?' Judd had asked.

Anne had turned her incredible violet eyes on him. 'No. I wasn't looking for a father figure. I had a very happy home life as a child.'

'Where were you born?'

'In Revere, a small town near Boston.'

'Are both your parents still alive?'

'Father is alive. Mother died of a stroke when I was twelve.'

'Did your father and mother have a good relationship?'

'Yes. They were very much in love.'

It shows in you, thought Judd happily. With all the sickness and aberration and misery that he had seen, having Anne here was like a breath of April freshness.

'Any brothers or sisters?'

'No. I was an only child. A spoiled brat.' She smiled up at him. It was an open, friendly smile without guile or affectation.

She told him that she had lived abroad with her father, who was serving in the State Department, and when he had remarried and moved to California, she had gone to work at the UN as an interpreter. She spoke fluent French, Italian, and Spanish. She had met her future husband in the Bahamas when she was on vacation. He owned a construction firm. Anne had not been attracted to him at first, but he had been a persistent and persuasive suitor. Two months after they met, Anne had married him. She had now been married for six months. They lived on an estate in New Jersey.

And that was all Judd had been able to find out about her in half a dozen visits. He still had not the slightest clue as to what her problem was. She had an emotional block about discussing it. He remembered some of the questions he had asked her during their first session.

'Does your problem involve your husband, Mrs Blake?'

No answer.

'Are you and your husband compatible, physically?'

'Yes.' Embarrassed.

'Do you suspect him of having an affair with another woman?'

'No.' Amused.

'Are you having an affair with another man?'

'No.' Angry.

He hesitated, trying to figure out the best approach to take to break down the barrier. He decided on a buckshot technique: he would touch on every major category until he struck a nerve.

'Do you quarrel about money?'

'No. He's very generous.'

'Any in-law problems?'

'He's an orphan. My father lives in California.'

'Were you or your husband ever addicted to drugs?'

'No.'

'Do you suspect your husband of being homosexual?'

A low, warm laugh. 'No.'

He pressed on, because he had to. 'Have you ever had a sexual relationship with a woman?'

'No.' Reproachful.

He had touched on alcoholism, frigidity, a pregnancy she was afraid to face – everything he could think of.

And each time she had looked at him with her thoughtful, intelligent eyes and had merely shaken her head. Whenever he tried to pin her down, she would head him off with, 'Please be patient with me. Let me do it my own way.'

With anyone else, he might have given up. But he knew that he had to help her. And he had to keep seeing her.

He had let her talk about any subject she chose. She had travelled to a dozen countries with her father and had met fascinating people. She had a quick mind and an unexpected humour. He found that they liked the same books, the same music, the same playwrights. She was warm and friendly, but Judd could never detect the slightest sign that she reacted to him as anything other than a doctor. It was bitter irony. He had been subconsciously searching for someone like Anne for years, and now that she had walked into his life, his job was to help her solve whatever her problem was and send her back to her husband.

Now, as Anne walked into the office. Judd moved to the chair next to the couch and waited for her to lie down.

'Not today,' she said quietly. 'I just came to see if I could help.'

He stared at her, speechless for a moment. His emotions had been stretched so tight in the past two days that her unexpected sympathy unnerved him. As he looked at her, he had a wild impulse to pour out everything that was happening to him. To tell her about the nightmare that was engulfing him, about McGreavy and his idiotic suspicions. But he knew he could not. He was the doctor and she was his patient. Worse than that. He was in love with her, and she was the untouchable wife of a man he did not even know.

She was standing there, watching him. He nodded, not trusting himself to speak.

'I liked Carol so much,' said Anne. 'Why would anyone kill her?'

'I don't know,' said Judd.

'Don't the police have any idea who did it?'

Do they? Judd thought bitterly. *If she only knew.*

Anne was looking at him curiously.

'The police have some theories,' Judd said.

'I know how terrible you must feel. I just wanted to come and tell you how very sorry I am. I wasn't even sure you'd be in the office today.'

'I wasn't going to come in,' Judd said. 'But – well, here I am. As long as we're both here, why don't we talk a little about you?'

Anne hesitated. 'I'm not sure that there's anything to talk about any more.'

Judd felt his heart jump. *Please, God, don't let her say that I'm not going to see her any more.*

'I'm going to Europe with my husband next week.'

'That's wonderful,' he made himself say.

'I'm afraid I've wasted your time, Dr Stevens, and I apologize.'

'Please don't,' Judd said. He found that his voice was husky. She was walking out on him. But of course she couldn't know that. He was being infantile. His mind told him this clinically while his stomach ached with the physical hurt of her going away. For ever.

She opened her purse and took out some money. She was in the habit of paying cash after each visit, unlike his other patients, who sent him cheques.

'No,' said Judd quickly. 'You came here as a friend. I'm grateful.'

Judd did something he had never done before with a patient. 'I would like you to come back once more,' he said.

She looked up at him quietly. 'Why?'

Because I can't bear to let you go so soon, he thought. *Because I'll never meet anyone like you again. Because I wish I had met you first. Because I love you.* Aloud he said, 'I thought we might – round things out. Talk a little to make sure that you really are over your problem.'

She smiled mischievously. 'You mean you want me to come back for my graduation?'

'Something like that,' he said. 'Will you do it?'

'If you want me to – of course.' She rose. 'I haven't given you a chance with me. But I know you're a wonderful doctor. If I should ever need help, I'd come to you.'

She held out her hand and he took it. She had a warm firm handclasp. He felt again that compelling current that ran between them and marvelled that she felt nothing.

'I'll see you Friday,' she said.

'Friday.'

He watched her walk out the private door leading to the corridor, then sank into a chair. He had never felt so completely alone in his life. But he couldn't sit here and do nothing. There had to be an answer, and if McGreavy wasn't going to find it, *he* had to discover it before McGreavy destroyed him. On the dark side, Lieutenant McGreavy suspected him of two murders that he couldn't prove he did not commit. He might be arrested at any moment, which would mean that his professional life would be destroyed. He was in love with a married woman he would only see once more. He forced himself to turn to the bright side. He couldn't think of a single bloody thing.

Chapter Five

The rest of the day went by as though he were under water. A few of the patients made reference to Carol's murder, but the more disturbed ones were so self-absorbed that they could only think of themselves and their problems. Judd tried to concentrate, but his thoughts kept drifting away, trying to find answers to what had happened. He would go over the tapes later to pick up what he had missed.

At seven o'clock, when Judd had ushered out the last patient, he went over to the recessed liquor cabinet and poured himself a stiff scotch. It hit him with a jolt, and he suddenly remembered that he had not had any breakfast or lunch. The thought of food made him ill. He sank into a chair and thought about the two murders. There was nothing in the case histories of any of his patients that would cause someone to commit murder. A blackmailer might have tried to steal them. But blackmailers were cowards, preying on the weaknesses of others, and if Carol had caught one breaking in and he had killed her, it would have been done quickly, with a single blow. He would not have tortured her. There had to be some other explanation.

Judd sat there a long time, his mind slowly sifting the events of the past two days. Finally, he sighed and gave it up. He looked at the clock and was startled to see how late it was.

By the time he left his office, it was after nine o'clock. As he stepped out of the lobby into the street, a blast of icy wind hit him. It had started to snow again. The snow swirled through the sky, gently blurring everything so that it looked as though the city had been painted on a canvas that had not dried and the paints were running, melting down skyscrapers and streets into watery greys and whites. A large red-and-white sign in a store window across the street on Lexington Avenue warned: Christmas. He resolutely turned his thoughts away from it and started to walk.

The street was deserted except for a lone pedestrian in the distance, hurrying home to his wife or sweetheart. Judd found himself wondering what Anne was doing. She was probably at home with her husband, discussing his day at the office, interested, caring. Or they had gone to bed, and . . . *Stop it!* he told himself.

There were no cars on the windswept street, so just before he reached the corner, Judd began to cross at an angle, heading towards the garage where he parked his car during the day. As he reached the middle of the street, he heard a noise behind him, and turned. A large black limousine without lights was coming towards him, its tyres fighting for traction in the light powder of snow. It was less than ten feet away. *The drunken fool*, thought Judd. *He's in a skid and he's going to kill himself.* Judd turned and leaped back towards the kerb and safety. The nose of the car swerved towards him, the car accelerating. Too late Judd realized the car was deliberately trying to run him down.

The last thing he remembered was something hard smashing against his chest, and a loud crash that sounded like thunder. The dark street suddenly lit up with bright Roman candles that seemed to explode in his head. In that split second of illumination, Judd suddenly knew the answer to everything. He knew why John Hanson and Carol Roberts had been murdered. He felt a sense of wild elation. He had to tell McGreavy. Then the light faded, and there was only the silence of the wet darkness.

From the outside, the Nineteenth Police Precinct looked like an ancient weatherbeaten four-storey school building: brown brick, plaster façade, and cornices white with the droppings of generations of pigeons. The Nineteenth Precinct was responsible for the area of Manhattan from Fifty-ninth Street to Eighty-sixth Street, from Fifth Avenue to the East River.

The call from the hospital reporting the hit-and-run accident came through the police switchboard a few minutes after ten and was transferred to the Detective Bureau. The Nineteenth Precinct was having a busy night. Because of the weather, there had been a heavy increase in rapes and muggings. The deserted streets had become a frozen wasteland where marauders preyed on the hapless stragglers who wandered into their territory.

Most of the detectives were out on squeals, and the Detective Bureau was deserted except for Detective Frank Angeli and a sergeant, who was interrogating an arson suspect.

When the phone rang, Angeli answered it. It was a nurse who had a hit-and-run patient at the city hospital. The patient was asking for Lieutenant McGreavy. McGreavy had gone to the Hall of Records. When she gave Angeli the name of the patient, he told the nurse that he would be right over.

Angeli was hanging up the receiver as McGreavy walked in. Angeli quickly told him about the call. 'We'd better get right over to the hospital,' Angeli said.

'He'll keep. First I want to talk to the captain of the precinct where that accident occurred.'

Angeli watched as McGreavy dialled the number. He wondered whether Captain Bertelli had told McGreavy about his conversation with Angeli. It had been short and to the point.

'Lieutenant McGreavy is a good cop,' Angeli had said, 'but I think he's influenced by what happened five years ago.'

Captain Bertelli had given him a long, cold stare. 'Are you accusing him of framing Dr Stevens?'

'I'm not accusing him of anything, Captain. I just thought you should be aware of the situation.'

'Okay, I'm aware of it.' And the meeting was over.

McGreavy's phone conversation took three minutes while McGreavy grunted and made notes and Angeli impatiently paced back and forth. Ten minutes later the two detectives were in a squad car on the way to the hospital.

Judd's room was on the sixth floor at the end of a long, dreary corridor that had the sickly-sweet smell of all hospitals. The nurse who had phoned was escorting them to Judd's room.

'What shape is he in, Nurse?' asked McGreavy.

'The doctor will have to tell you that,' she said primly. And then continued, compulsively. 'It's a miracle the man wasn't killed. He has a possible concussion, some bruised ribs, and an injured left arm.'

'Is he conscious?' asked Angeli.

'Yes. We're having a terrible time keeping him in bed.' She turned to McGreavy. 'He keeps saying he has to see you.'

They walked into the room. There were six beds in the room, all occupied. The nurse indicated a bed at the far corner that was curtained off, and McGreavy and Angeli walked over to it and stepped behind the curtain.

Judd was in bed, propped up. His face was pale and there was a large adhesive plaster on his forehead. His left arm was in a sling.

McGreavy spoke. 'I hear you had an accident.'

'It wasn't an accident,' said Judd. 'Someone tried to kill me.' His voice was weak and shaky.

'Who?' asked Angeli.

'I don't know, but it all fits in.' He turned to McGreavy. 'The killers weren't after John Hanson or Carol. They were after me.'

McGreavy looked at him in surprise. 'What makes you think so?'

'Hanson was killed because he was wearing my yellow slicker. They must have seen me go into my building wearing that coat. When Hanson came out of my office wearing it, they mistook him for me.'

'That's possible,' said Angeli.

'Sure,' said McGreavy. He turned to Judd. 'And when they learned that they had killed the wrong man, they came into your office and tore your clothes off and found out you were really a coloured girl, and they got so mad they beat you to death.'

'Carol was killed because they found her there when they came to get me,' Judd said.

McGreavy reached in his overcoat pocket and took out some notes. 'I just talked to the captain of the precinct where the accident happened.'

'It was no accident.'

'According to the police report, you were jay-walking.'

Judd stared at him. 'Jaywalking?' he repeated weakly.

'You crossed in the middle of the street, Doctor.'

'There were no cars so I – '

'There *was* a car,' McGreavy corrected. 'Only you didn't see it. It was snowing and the visibility was lousy. You stepped out of nowhere. The driver put on his brakes, went into a skid, and hit you. Then he panicked and drove away.'

'That's not the way it happened and his headlights were off.'

'And you think *that's* evidence that he killed Hanson and Carol Roberts?'

'Someone tried to kill me,' repeated Judd insistently.

McGreavy shook his head. 'It won't work, Doctor.'

'What won't work?' asked Judd.

'Did you really expect me to start beating the bushes for some mythical killer while you take the heat off yourself?' His voice was suddenly hard. 'Did you know your receptionist was pregnant?'

Judd closed his eyes and let his head sink back on the pillow. So that was what Carol had wanted to speak to him about. He had half-guessed. And now McGreavy would think . . . He opened his eyes. 'No,' he said wearily. 'I didn't.'

Judd's head began pounding again. The pain was returning. He swallowed to fight off the nausea that engulfed him. He wanted to ring for the nurse, but he was damned if he would give McGreavy the satisfaction.

'I went through the records at City Hall,' said McGreavy. 'What would you say if I told you that your cute little pregnant receptionist had been a hooker before she went to work for you?' The pounding in Judd's head was becoming steadily worse. 'Were you aware of that, Dr Stevens? You don't have to answer. I'll answer for you. You knew it because you picked her up in night court four years ago, when she was arrested on a charge of soliciting. Now isn't it a little far-out for a respectable doctor to hire a hooker as a receptionist in a high-class office?'

'No one is born a hooker,' said Judd. 'I was trying to help a sixteen-year-old child have a chance in life.'

'And get yourself a little free black tail on the side?'

'You dirty-minded bastard!'

McGreavy smiled without mirth. 'Where did you take Carol after you found her in night court?'

'To my apartment.'

'And she slept there?'

'Yes.'

McGreavy grinned. 'You're a beauty! You picked up a good-looking young whore in night court and took her to your apartment to spend the night. What were you looking for – a chess partner? If you really didn't sleep with her, there's a damn good chance you're a homosexual. And guess who that ties you in with?

65

Right. John Hanson. If you *did* sleep with Carol, then the chances are pretty good that you continued sleeping with her until you finally got her knocked up. And you have the gall to lie there and tell me some cock-and-bull story about a hit-and-run maniac who's going around murdering people?' McGreavy turned and strode out of the room, his face red with anger.

The pounding in Judd's head had turned to a throbbing agony.

Angeli was watching him, worried. 'You all right?'

'You've got to help me,' Judd said. 'Someone is trying to kill me.' It sounded like a threnody in his ears.

'Who'd have a motive for killing you, Doctor?'

'I don't know.'

'Do you have any enemies?'

'No.'

'Have you been sleeping with anyone's wife or girl friend?'

Judd shook his head and instantly regretted the motion.

'Is there any money in your family – relatives who might want to get you out of the way?'

'No.'

Angeli sighed. 'Okay. So there's no motive for anyone wanting to murder you. What about your patients? I think you'd better give us a list so we can check them out.'

'I can't do that.'

'All I'm asking for is their names.'

'I'm sorry.' It was an effort to speak. 'If I were a dentist or a chiropodist I'd give it to you. But don't you see? These people have problems. Most of them

66

serious problems. If you started questioning them, you'd not only shatter them; you'd destroy their confidence in me. I wouldn't be able to treat them any more. I can't give you that list.' He lay back on the pillow, exhausted.

Angeli looked at him quietly, then asked, 'What do you call a man who thinks that everyone's out to kill him?'

'A paranoiac,' said Judd. He saw the look on Angeli's face. 'You don't think I'm . . . ?'

'Put yourself in my place,' Angeli said. 'If I were in that bed right now, talking like you, and you were my doctor, what would you think?'

Judd closed his eyes against the stabs of pain in his head. He heard Angeli's voice continue. 'McGreavy's waiting for me.'

Judd opened his eyes. 'Wait . . . Give me a chance to prove that I'm telling the truth.'

'How?'

'Whoever's trying to kill me is going to try again. I want someone with me. Next time they try, he can catch them.'

Angeli looked at Judd. 'Dr Stevens, if someone really wants to kill you, all the policemen in the world can't stop them. If they don't get you today, they'll get you tomorrow. If they don't get you here, they'll get you somewhere else. It doesn't matter whether you're a king or a president, or just plain John Doe. Life is a very thin thread. It only takes a second to snap it.'

'There's nothing – nothing at all you can do?'

'I can give you some advice. Have new locks put on the doors of your apartment, and check the windows to make sure they're securely bolted. Don't let anyone in the apartment unless you know them. No delivery boys unless you've ordered the delivery yourself.'

Judd nodded, his throat dry and aching.

'Your building has a doorman and an elevator man,' continued Angeli. 'Can you trust them?'

'The doorman has worked there for ten years. The elevator operator has been there eight years. I'd trust them with my life.'

Angeli nodded approvingly. 'Good. Ask them to keep their eyes open. If they're on the alert, it's going to be hard for anyone to sneak up to your apartment. What about the office? Are you going to hire a new receptionist?'

Judd thought of a stranger sitting at Carol's desk, in her chair. A spasm of helpless anger wracked him. 'Not right away.'

'You might think about hiring a man,' said Angeli.

'I'll think about it.'

Angeli turned to go, then stopped. 'I have an idea,' he said hesitantly, 'but it's a long shot.'

'Yes?' He hated the eagerness in his voice.

'This man who killed McGreavy's old partner . . .'

'Ziffren.'

'Was he really insane?'

'Yes. They sent him to the Matteawan State Hospital for mentally ill criminals.'

'Maybe he blames you for having him put away. I'll check him out. Just to make sure he hasn't escaped or been released. Give me a call in the morning.'

'Thanks,' Judd said gratefully.

'It's my job. If you're involved in any of this, I'm

68

going to help McGreavy nail you.' Angeli turned to go. He stopped again. 'You don't have to mention to McGreavy that I'm checking on Ziffren for you.'

'I won't.'

The two men smiled at each other. Angeli left. Judd was alone again.

If the situation was bleak that morning it was even bleaker now. Judd knew that he would already have been arrested for murder except for one thing – McGreavy's character. McGreavy wanted vengeance and he wanted it so badly that he would make sure that every last bit of evidence was in place. *Could* the hit-and-run have been an accident? There had been snow on the street, and the limousine could have accidentally skidded into him. But then, why had the headlights been off? And where had the car come from so suddenly?

He was convinced now that an assassin had struck – and would strike again. With that thought, he fell asleep.

Early the next morning Peter and Norah Hadley came to the hospital to see Judd. They had heard about the accident on the morning news.

Peter was Judd's age, smaller than Judd and painfully thin. They had come from the same town in Nebraska and had gone through medical school together.

Norah was English. She was blonde and chubby with a large, soft bosom a bit too large for her five feet three inches. She was vivacious and comfortable, and after five minutes' conversation with her, people felt they had known her for ever.

'You look lousy,' Peter said, studying Judd critically.

'That's what I like, Doctor. A bedside manner.' Judd's headache was almost gone and the pain in his body had been reduced to a dull, aching soreness.

Norah handed him a bouquet of carnations. 'We brought you some flowers, love,' she said. 'You poor old darling.' She leaned over and kissed him on the cheek.

'How did it happen?' asked Peter.

Judd hesitated. 'It was a hit-and-run accident.'

'Everything hit the fan at once, didn't it? I read about poor Carol.'

'It's dreadful,' said Norah. 'I liked her so much.'

Judd felt a tightness in his throat. 'So did I.'

'Any chance of catching the bastard who did it?' Peter asked.

'They're working on it.'

'In this morning's paper it said that a Lieutenant McGreavy is close to making an arrest. Do you know anything about it?'

'A little,' Judd said dryly. 'McGreavy likes to keep me up to date.'

'You never know how wonderful the police are until you really need them,' Norah said.

'Dr Harris let me take a look at your X-rays. Some nasty bruises – no concussion. You'll be out of here in a few days.'

But Judd knew he had no time to spare.

They spent the next half hour in small talk, carefully avoiding the subject of Carol Roberts. Peter and Norah were unaware that John Hanson had been a patient of Judd's. For some reason of his own, McGreavy had kept that part of the story out of the newspapers.

When they got up to leave, Judd asked to speak to Peter alone. While Norah waited outside, Judd told Peter about Harrison Burke.

'I'm sorry,' said Peter. 'When I sent him to you, I knew he was in a bad way, but I was hoping there was still time for you to help him. Of course you have to put him away. When are you going to do it?'

'As soon as I get out of here,' Judd said. And he knew he was lying. He didn't want Harrison Burke sent away. Not just yet. He wanted to find out first whether Burke could have committed the two murders.

'If there's anything I can do for you, old buddy – call.' And Peter was gone.

Judd lay there, planning his next move. Since there was no rational motive for anyone wanting to kill him, it stood to reason that the murders had been committed by someone who was mentally unbalanced, someone with an imagined grievance against him. The only two people he could think of who might fit into that category were Harrison Burke and Amos Ziffren, the man who had killed McGreavy's partner. If Burke had no alibi for the morning Hanson was killed, then Judd would ask Detective Angeli to check him out further. If Burke had an alibi, then he would concentrate on Ziffren. The feeling of depression that had enveloped him began to lift. He felt that at last he was doing something. He was suddenly desperately impatient to get out of the hospital.

He rang for the nurse and told her he wanted to see Dr Harris. Ten minutes later Seymour Harris walked into the room. He was a little gnome of a man with bright blue eyes and tufts of black hair sticking out of his cheeks. Judd had known him a long time and had a great respect for him.

'Well! Sleeping Beauty's awake. You look terrible.'

Judd was getting tired of hearing it. 'I feel fine,' he lied. 'I want to get out of here.'

'When?'

'Now.'

Dr Harris looked at him reprovingly. 'You just got here. Why don't you stick around a few days? I'll send you in a few nymphomaniac nurses to keep you company.'

'Thanks, Seymour. I really do have to leave.'

Dr Harris sighed. 'Okay. You're the doctor, Doctor. Personally, I wouldn't let my cat walk around in your condition.' He looked at Judd keenly. 'Anything I can do to help?'

Judd shook his head.

'I'll have Miss Bedpan get your clothes.'

Thirty minutes later the girl at the reception desk called a taxi for him. He was at his office at ten-fifteen.

Chapter Six

His first patient, Teri Washburn, was waiting in the corridor. Twenty years earlier Teri had been one of the biggest stars in the Hollywood firmament. Her career had fizzled overnight, and she had married a lumberman from Oregon and dropped out of sight. Teri had been married five or six times since then and was now living in New York with her latest husband, an importer. She looked up angrily as Judd came down the corridor.

'Well . . .' she said. The speech of reproval she had rehearsed died away as she saw his face. 'What happened to you?' she asked. 'You look like you got caught between two horny mix-masters.'

'Just a little accident. Sorry I'm late.' He unlocked the door and ushered Teri into the reception office. Carol's empty desk and chair loomed in front of him.

'I read about Carol,' Teri said. There was an excited edge to her voice. 'Was it a sex murder?'

'No,' Judd said shortly. He opened the door to his inner office. 'Give me ten minutes.'

He went into the office, consulted his calendar pad, and began dialling the numbers of his patients, cancelling the rest of his appointments for the day. He was able to reach all but three patients. His chest and arm hurt every time he moved, and his head was beginning to pound again. He took two Darvan from a drawer and washed them down with a glass of water. He walked over to the reception door and opened it for Teri. He steeled himself to put everything out of his mind for the next fifty minutes except the problems of his patient. Teri lay down on the couch, her skirt hiked up, and began talking.

Twenty years ago Teri Washburn had been a raving beauty, and traces of it were still there. She had the largest, softest, most innocent eyes that Judd had ever seen. The sultry mouth had a few hard lines around it, but it was still voluptuous, and her breasts were rounded and firm beneath a close-fitting Pucci print. Judd suspected that she had had a silicone injection, but he was waiting for her to mention it. The rest of her body was still good, and her legs were great.

At one time or another, most of Judd's female patients thought they were in love with him, the natural transference from patient-doctor to patient-protector-lover. But Teri's case was different. She had been trying to have an affair with Judd from the first minute she had walked into his office. She had tried to arouse him in every way she could think of – and Teri was an expert. Judd had finally warned her that unless she behaved herself, he would send her to another doctor. Since then she had behaved reasonably well with him: studying him, trying to find his Achilles heel. An eminent English physician had sent Teri to him after a nasty international scandal at Antibes. A French gossip columnist had accused Teri of spending a weekend on the yacht of a famour Greek shipping magnate to whom she was engaged, and sleeping with his three brothers while the ship's owner flew to Rome for a day on business. The story was quickly hushed up and the columnist printed a retraction and was then quietly fired. In her first session with Judd, Teri had boasted that the story was true.

'It's wild,' she had said. 'I need sex all the time. I can't get enough of it.' She had rubbed her hands against her hips, sliding her skirt up, and looked at Judd innocently. 'Do you know what I mean, honey?' she had asked.

Since that first visit, Judd had found out a great deal about Teri. She had come from a small coal-mining town in Pennsylvania.

'My father was a dumb Polack. He got his kicks getting drunk on boilermakers every Saturday night and beating the shit out of my old lady.'

When she was thirteen, Teri had the body of a woman and the face of an angel. She learned that she could earn nickels by going to the back of the coal tips with the miners. The day her father had found out, he had come into their small cabin screaming incoherently in Polish, and had thrown Teri's mother out. He had locked the door, taken off his heavy belt, and begun beating Teri. When he was through, he had raped her.

Judd had watched Teri as she lay there describing the scene, her face empty of any emotion.

'That was the last time I saw my father or mother.'

'You ran away,' Judd said.

Teri twisted around on the couch in surprise. 'What?'

'After your father raped you – '

'Ran away?' Teri said. She threw back her head and let out a whoop of laughter. 'I *liked* it. It was my bitch of a mother who threw me out!'

Now Judd switched on the tape recorder. 'What would you like to talk about?' he asked.

'Fucking,' she said. 'Why don't we psychoanalyse you and find out why you're so straight?'

He ignored it. 'Why did you think Carol's death might have something to do with a sexual attack?'

'Because everything reminds me of sex, honey.' She squirmed and her skirt rode a little higher.

'Pull your skirt down, Teri.'

She gave him an innocent look. 'Sorry . . . You missed a great birthday party Saturday night, Doc.'

'Tell me about it.'

She hesitated, an unaccustomed note of concern in her voice. 'You won't hate me?'

'I've told you that you don't need my approval. The only one whose approval you need is you. Right and wrong are the rules we make up ourselves so that we can play in the game with other people. Without rules, there can't be a game. But never forget – the rules are artificial.'

There was a silence. Then she spoke. 'It was a swinging party. My husband hired a six-piece band.'

He waited.

She twisted around to look at him. 'Are you sure you won't lose respect for me?'

'I want to help you. We've all done things we're ashamed of, but that does not signify that we have to continue doing them.'

She studied him a moment, then lay back on the couch. 'Did I ever tell you I suspected my husband, Harry, is impotent?'

'Yes.' She talked of it constantly.

'He hasn't really done it to me since we've been married. He always has some goddamn excuse . . . Well . . .' Her mouth twisted bitterly. 'Well . . .

Saturday night I fucked the band while Harry watched.'
She began to cry.

Judd handed her some Kleenex and sat there,
watching her.

No one had ever given Teri Washburn anything in
her life that she had not been overcharged for. When
she had first gone to Hollywood, she had landed a
job as a waitress in a drive-in and used most of
her wages to go to a third-rate dramatic coach.
Within a week the coach had her move in with him,
doing all his household chores and confining her
coaching to the bedroom. A few weeks later, when she
realized that he could not have got her an acting job
even if he had wanted to, she had walked out on him
and taken a job as a cashier in a Beverly Hills
hotel drugstore. A movie executive had appeared on
Christmas Eve to buy a last-minute gift for his wife.
He had given Teri his card and told her to call him.
Teri had made a screen test a week later. She was
awkward and untrained, but she had three things going
for her. She had a sensational face and figure, the
camera loved her, and the studio executive was keeping
her.

Teri Washburn appeared in bit parts in a dozen
pictures the first year. She began to get fan mail. Her
parts grew larger. At the end of a year her benefactor
died of a heart attack, and Teri was afraid the studio
would fire her. Instead, the new executive called her in
and told her that he had big plans for her. She got a new
contract, a raise, and a larger apartment with a
mirrored bedroom. Teri's roles gradually grew to leads
in B pictures, and finally, as the public showed their
adoration by putting down their money at the box office

to see each new Teri Washburn picture, she began to star in A pictures.

All that had been a long time ago, and Judd felt sorry for her as she lay on his couch, trying to control her sobs.

'Would you like some water?' he asked.

'N-no,' she said, 'I'm f-fine.' She took a handkerchief out of her purse and blew her nose. 'I'm sorry,' she said, 'for behaving like a goddamn idiot.' She sat up.

Judd sat there quietly, waiting for her to get control of herself.

'Why do I marry men like Harry?'

'That's an important question. Do you have any idea why?'

'How the hell should I know!' screamed Teri. 'You're the psychiatrist. If I knew they were like that, you don't think I'd marry those creeps, do you?'

'What do you think?'

She stared at him, shocked. 'You mean you think I *would*?' She got to her feet angrily. 'Why, you dirty sonofabitch! You think I *liked* fucking the band?'

'Did you?'

In a fury she picked up a vase and flung it at him. It shattered against a table. 'Does that answer you?'

'No. That vase was two hundred dollars. I'll put it on your bill.'

She stared at him helplessly. 'Did I really like it?' she whispered.

'You tell me.'

Her voice dropped even lower. 'I must be sick,' she said. 'Oh, God, I'm sick. Please help me, Judd. Help me!'

Judd walked over to her. 'You've got to help me help you.'

She nodded her head, dumbly.

'I want you to go home and think about how you feel, Teri. Not while you're doing these things, but before you do them. Think about why you want to do them. When you know that, you'll know a great deal about yourself.'

She looked at him a moment, then her face relaxed. She took out her handkerchief and blew her nose again. 'You're a helluva man, Charlie Brown,' she said. She picked up her purse and gloves. 'See you next week?'

'Yes.' he said. 'See you next week.' He opened the door to the corridor, and Teri exited.

He knew the answer to Teri's problem, but she would have to work it through for herself. She would have to learn that she could not buy love, that it had to be given freely. And she could not accept the fact that it could be given to her freely until she learned to believe that she was worthy of receiving love. Until that time, Teri would go on trying to buy it, using the only currency she had: her body. He knew the agony she was going through, the bottomless despair of self-loathing, and his heart went out to her. But the only way in which he could help her was to give the appearance of being impersonal and detached. He knew that to his patients he seemed remote and aloof from their problems, dispensing wisdom from some Olympian height. But that was a vital part of the façade of therapy. In reality he cared deeply about the problems of his patients. They would have been amazed if they had known how often the unspeakable demons that tried to batter down the ramparts of their emotions appeared in Judd's own nightmares.

During the first six months of his practice as a psychiatrist, when he was undergoing the required two years of analysis necessary to become a psychoanalyst, Judd had developed blinding headaches. He was empathetically taking on the symptoms of all his patients, and it had taken him almost a year to learn to channel and control his emotional involvement.

Now, as Judd locked Teri Washburn's tape away, his mind came forcibly back to his own dilemma. He walked over to the phone and dialled information for the number of the Nineteenth Precinct.

The switchboard operator connected him with the Detective Bureau. He heard McGreavy's deep bass voice over the phone, 'Lieutenant McGreavy.'

'Detective Angeli, please.'

'Hold on.'

Judd heard the clatter of the phone as McGreavy put the receiver down. A moment later Angeli's voice came over the wire. 'Detective Angeli.'

'Judd Stevens. I wondered whether you'd got that information yet?'

There was an instant's hesitation. 'I checked into it,' said Angeli carefully.

'All you have to do is say "yes" or "no".' Judd's heart was pounding. It was an effort for him to ask the next question. 'Is Ziffren still at Matteawan?'

It seemed an eternity before Angeli answered. 'Yes. He's still there.'

A wave of disappointment surged through Judd. 'Oh. I see.'

'I'm sorry.'

80

'Thanks,' Judd said. Slowly he hung up.

So that left Harrison Burke. Harrison Burke, a hopeless paranoiac who was convinced that everyone was out to kill him. Had Burke decided to strike first? John Hanson had left Judd's office at ten-fifty on Monday and had been killed a few minutes later. Judd had to find out whether Harrison Burke was in his office at that time. He looked up Burke's office number and dialled it.

'International Steel.' The voice had the remote, impersonal timbre of an automaton.

'Mr Harrison Burke, please.'

'Mr Harrison Burke . . . Thank you . . . One moment, please . . .'

Judd was gambling on Burke's secretary answering the phone. If she had stepped out for a moment and Burke answered it himself . . . 'Mr Burke's office.' It was a girl's voice.

'This is Dr Judd Stevens. I wonder if you could give me some information?'

'Oh, yes, Dr Stevens!' There was a note of relief in her voice, mixed with apprehension. She must have known that Judd was Burke's analyst. Was she counting on him for help? What had Burke been doing to upset her?

'It's about Mr Burke's bill . . .' Judd began.

'His *bill*?' She made no effort to conceal her disappointment.

Judd went on quickly. 'My receptionist is – is no longer with me, and I'm trying to straighten out the books. I see that she charged Mr Burke for a nine-thirty appointment this past Monday, and I wonder if you'd mind checking his calendar for that morning?'

'Just a moment,' she said. There was disapproval in her voice now. He could read her mind. Her employer was cracking up and his analyst was only concerned about getting his money. She came back on the phone a few minutes later. 'I'm afraid your receptionist made a mistake, Dr Stevens,' she said tartly. 'Mr Burke couldn't have been at your office Monday morning.'

'Are you sure?' persisted Judd. 'It's down in her book – nine-thirty to – '

'I don't care what's down in her book, Doctor.' She was angry now, upset by his callousness. 'Mr Burke was in a staff meeting all morning on Monday. It began at eight o'clock.'

'Couldn't he have slipped out for an hour?'

'No, Doctor,' she said. 'Mr Burke never leaves his office during the day.' There was an accusation in her voice. *Can't you see that he's ill? What are you doing to help him?*

'Shall I tell him you called?'

'That won't be necessary,' Judd said. 'Thank you.' He wanted to add a word of reassurance, of comfort, but there was nothing he could say. He hung up.

So that was that. He had struck out. If neither Ziffren nor Harrison Burke had tried to kill him – then there could be no one else with any motive. He was back where he had started. Some person – or persons – had murdered his receptionist and one of his patients. The hit-and-run incident could have been deliberate or accidental. At the time it happened, it seemed to be deliberate. But looking at it dispassionately, Judd admitted to himself that he had been wrought up by the events of the last few days. In his highly emotional state he could easily have turned an accident into something sinister. The simple truth was that there was no one who could have any possible motive for killing him. He had an excellent relationship with all his patients, warm relationships with his friends. He had never, to his knowledge, harmed anyone. The phone rang. He recognized Anne's low, throaty voice instantly.

'Are you busy?'

'No. I can talk.'

There was concern in her voice. 'I read that you were hit by a car. I wanted to call you sooner, but I didn't know where to reach you.'

He made his voice light. 'It was nothing serious. It will teach me not to jaywalk.'

'The papers said it was a hit-and-run accident.'

'Yes.'

'Did they find the person who did it?'

'No. It was probably some kid out for a lark.' *In a black limousine without lights.*

'Are you sure?' asked Anne.

The question caught him by surprise. 'What do you mean?'

'I don't really know.' Her voice was uncertain. 'It's just that – Carol was murdered. And now – this.'

So she had put it together, too.

'It – it almost sounds as if there's a maniac running around loose.'

'If there is,' Judd assured her, 'the police will catch him.'

'Are you in any danger?'

His heart warmed. 'Of course not.' There was an awkward silence. There was so much he wanted to say, but he couldn't. He must not mistake a friendly phone call for anything more than the natural concern that a patient would have for her doctor. Anne was the type who would have called anyone who was in trouble. It meant no more than that.

'I'll still see you on Friday?' he asked.

'Yes.' There was an odd note in her voice. Was she going to change her mind?

'It's a date,' he said quickly. But of course it was not a date. It was a business appointment.

'Yes. Goodbye, Dr Stevens.'

'Goodbye, Mrs Blake. Thanks for calling. Thanks very much.' He hung up. And thought about Anne. And wondered if her husband had any idea what an incredibly lucky man he was.

What was her husband like? In the little Anne had said about him, Judd had formed the image of an attractive and thoughtful man. He was a sportsman, bright, was a successful businessman, donated money to the arts. He sounded like the kind of person Judd would have liked for a friend. Under different circumstances.

What could Anne's problem have been that she was afraid to discuss with her husband? Or her analyst? With a person of Anne's character, it was probably an overwhelming feeling of guilt because of an affair she had had either before she was married or after her marriage. He could not imagine her having casual affairs. Perhaps she would tell him on Friday. When he saw her for the last time.

The rest of the afternoon went by swiftly. Judd saw the few patients he had not been able to cancel. When the last one had departed, he took out the tape of Harrison Burke's last session and played it, making occasional notes as he listened.

When he had finished, he switched the tape recorder off. There was no choice. He had to call Burke's employer in the morning and inform him of Burke's condition. He glanced out of the window and was surprised to see that night had fallen. It was almost eight o'clock. Now that he had finished concentrating on his work, he suddenly felt stiff and tired. His ribs were sore and his arm had begun to throb. He would go home and soak in a nice hot bath.

He put away all the tapes except Burke's, which he locked in a drawer of a side table. He would turn it over to a court-appointed psychiatrist. He put on his overcoat and was halfway out the door when the phone rang. He went to the phone and picked it up. 'Dr Stevens.'

There was no answer on the other end. He heard breathing, heavy and nasal.

'Hello?'

There was no response. Judd hung up. He stood there a moment, frowning. Wrong number, he decided. He turned out the office lights, locked the doors, and moved towards the bank of elevators. All the tenants were long since gone. It was too early for the night shift of maintenance workers, and except for Bigelow, the watchman, the building was deserted.

Judd walked over to the elevator and pressed the call button. The signal indicator did not move. He pressed the button again. Nothing happened.

And at that moment all the lights in the corridor blacked out.

Chapter Seven

Judd stood in front of the elevator, the wave of darkness lapping at him like a physical force. He could feel his heart slow and then begin to beat faster. A sudden, atavistic fear flooded his body, and he reached in his pockets for a book of matches. He had left them in the office. Perhaps the lights were working on the floors below. Moving slowly and cautiously, he groped his way towards the door that led to the stairwell. He pushed the door open. The stairwell was in darkness. Carefully holding onto the railing, he started down into the blackness. In the distance below, he saw the wavering beam of a flashlight moving up the stairs. He was filled with a sudden relief. Bigelow, the watchman. 'Bigelow!' he yelled. 'Bigelow! It's Dr Stevens!' His voice bounced against the stone walls, echoing eerily through the stairwell. The figure holding the flashlight kept climbing silently, inexorably upward. 'Who's there?' Judd demanded. The only answer was the echo of his words.

And Judd suddenly knew who was there. His assassins. There had to be at least two of them. One had cut off the power in the basement while the other blocked the stairs to prevent his escape.

The beam of the flashlight was coming closer, only two or three floors below now, climbing rapidly. Judd's body went cold with fear. His heart began to pound like a trip-hammer, and his legs felt weak. He turned quickly and went back up the stairs to his floor. He opened the door and stood, listening. What if someone were waiting up here in the dark corridor for him?

The sounds of footsteps advancing up the stairs were louder now. His mouth dry, Judd turned and made his way along the inky corridor. When he reached the elevators, he began counting office doors. As he reached his office, he heard the stairwell door open. The keys slipped from his nervous fingers and dropped to the floor. He fumbled for them frantically, found them, opened the door to his reception room, and went in, double-locking the door behind him. No one could open it now without a special key.

From the corridor outside, he could hear the sound of approaching footsteps. He went into his private office and flicked the light switch. Nothing happened. There was no power at all in the building. He locked the inner door, then moved to the phone. He fumbled for the dial and dialled the operator. There were three long, steady rings, and then the operator's voice, Judd's only link to the outside world.

He spoke softly. 'Operator, this is an emergency. This is Dr Judd Stevens. I want to speak to Detective Frank Angeli at the Nineteenth Precinct. Please hurry!'

'Thank you. Your number please?'

Judd gave it to her.

'One moment, please.'

He heard the sound of someone testing the corridor entrance to his private office. They could not get in that way because there was no outside knob on the door.

'Hurry, Operator!'

'One moment, please,' replied the cool, unhurried voice.

There was a buzz on the line and then the police switchboard operator spoke. 'Nineteenth Precinct.'

Judd's heart leaped. 'Detective Angeli,' he said. 'It's urgent!'

'Detective Angeli ... just a moment, please.'

Outside in the corridor, something was happening. He could hear the sound of muted voices. Someone had joined the first man. What were they planning?

A familiar voice came on the phone. 'Detective Angeli's not here. This is his partner, Lieutenant McGreavy. Can – '

'This is Judd Stevens. I'm in my office. The lights are all out and someone's trying to break in and kill me!'

There was a heavy silence on the other end. 'Look, Doctor,' said McGreavy. 'Why don't you come down here and we'll talk a – '

'I can't come down there.' Judd almost shouted. 'Someone's trying to murder me!'

There was another silence at the other end of the line. McGreavy did not believe him and was not going to help him. Outside, Judd heard a door open, and then the sound of voices in the reception office. They were in the reception office! It was impossible for them to have got in without a key. But he could hear them moving, coming towards the door to his private office.

McGreavy's voice was coming over the phone, but Judd did not even listen. It was too late. He replaced the receiver. It would not have mattered even if McGreavy had agreed to come. The assassins were

88

here! *Life is a very thin thread and it only takes a second to snap it.* The fear that gripped him turned to a blind rage. He refused to be slaughtered like Hanson and Carol. He was going to put up a fight. He felt around in the dark for a possible weapon. An ashtray . . . a letter opener . . . useless. The assassins would have guns. It was a Kafka nightmare. He was being condemned for no reason by faceless executioners.

He heard them moving closer to the inner door and knew that he only had a minute or two left to live. With a strange, dispassionate calm, as though he were his own patient, he examined his final thoughts. He thought of Anne, and a sense of aching loss filled him. He thought of his patients, and of how much they needed him. Harrison Burke. With a pang he remembered that he had not yet told Burke's employer that Burke had to be committed. He would put the tapes where they could be . . . His heart lurched. Perhaps he *did* have a weapon to fight with!

He heard the doorknob turning. The door was locked, but it was flimsy. It would be simple for them to break in. He quickly groped his way in the dark to the table where he had locked away Burke's tape. He heard a creak as pressure was applied against the reception-room door. Then he heard someone fumbling at the lock. *Why don't they just break it down?* he thought. Somewhere, far back in his mind, he felt the answer was important, but he had no time to think about it now. With trembling fingers he unlocked the drawer with the tape in it. He ripped it out of its cardboard container, then moved over to the tape player and started to thread it. It was an outside chance, but it was the only one he had.

He stood there, concentrating, trying to recall his exact conversation with Burke. The pressure on the door increased. Judd gave a quick, silent prayer. 'I'm sorry about the power going out,' he said aloud. 'But I'm sure they'll have it fixed in a few minutes, Harrison. Why don't you lie down and relax?'

The noise at the door suddenly ceased. Judd had finished threading the tape into the player. He pressed the 'on' button. Nothing happened. Of course! All the power in the building was off. He could hear them begin to work on the lock again. A feeling of desperation seized him. 'That's better,' he said loudly. 'Just make yourself comfortable.' He fumbled for the packet of matches on the table, found it, tore out a match and lit it. He held the flame close to the tape player. There was a switch marked 'battery'. He turned the knob, then pressed the 'on' button again. At that moment, there was a sudden click as the lock on the door sprung open. His last defence was gone!

And then Burke's voice rang through the room. 'Is that all you've got to say? You don't even want to hear my proof. How do I know you're not one of them?'

Judd froze, not daring to move, his heart roaring like thunder.

'You know I'm not one of them,' said Judd's voice from the tape. 'I'm your friend. I'm trying to help you . . . Tell me about your proof.'

'They broke into my house last night,' Burke's voice said. 'They came to kill me. But I was too clever for them. I sleep in my den now, and I have extra locks on all the doors so they can't get to me.'

The sounds in the outer office had ceased.

Judd's voice again. 'Did you report the break-in to the police?'

'Of course not! The police are in it with them. They have orders to shoot me. But they wouldn't dare do it while there are other people around, so I stay in crowds.'

'I'm glad you gave me this information.'

'What are you going to do with it?'

'I'm listening very carefully to everything you say,' said Judd's voice. 'I've got it all down' – at that moment a warning screamed in Judd's brain; the next words were – 'on tape.'

He made a dive for the switch and pressed it. ' – in my mind,' Judd said loudly. 'And we'll work out the best way to handle it.' He stopped. He could not play the tape again because he had no way of telling where to pick it up. His only hope was that the men outside were convinced that Judd had a patient in the office with him. Even if they believed it, would it stop them?

'Cases like this,' Judd said, raising his voice, 'are really more common than you'd believe, Harrison.' He gave an impatient exclamation. 'I wish they'd get these lights back on. I know your chauffeur's waiting out in front for you. He'll probably wonder what's wrong and come up.'

Judd stopped and listened. He could hear whispering from the other side of the door. What were they deciding? From the distant street below, he suddenly heard the insistent wail of an approaching siren. The whispering stopped. He listened for the sound of the outer door closing, but he could hear nothing. Were they still out there, waiting? The scream of the siren grew louder. It stopped in front of the building.

And suddenly all the lights went on.

Chapter Eight

'Drink?'

McGreavy shook his head moodily, studying Judd. Judd poured himself his second stiff scotch while McGreavy watched without comment. Judd's hands were still trembling. As the warmth of the whisky floated through him, he felt himself beginning to relax.

McGreavy had arrived at the office two minutes after the lights had come on. With him was a stolid police sergeant who now sat making notes in a shorthand notebook.

McGreavy was talking. 'Let's go over it once more, Dr Stevens.'

Judd took a deep breath and began again, deliberately keeping his voice calm and low. 'I locked the office and went to the elevator. The corridor lights blacked out. I thought that the lights on the lower floors might be working, and I started to walk down.' Judd hesitated, reliving the fear. 'I saw someone coming up the stairs with a flashlight. I called out. I thought it was Bigelow, the guard. It wasn't.'

'Who was it?'

'I've told you,' said Judd. 'I don't know. They didn't answer.'

'What made you think they were coming to kill you?'

An angry retort came to Judd's lips, and he checked

it. It was essential to make McGreavy believe him. 'They followed me back to my office.'

'You think there were two men trying to kill you?'

'At least two,' Judd said. 'I heard them whispering.'

'You said that when you entered your reception office, you locked the outside door leading to the corridor. Is that right?'

'Yes.'

'And that when you came into your inner office, you locked the door leading to the reception office.'

'Yes.'

McGreavy walked over to the door leading from the reception office to Judd's inner office. 'Did they try to force this door?'

'No,' admitted Judd. He remembered how puzzled he had been by that.

'Right,' said McGreavy. 'When you lock the reception-office door that opens onto the corridor, it takes a special key to open it from the outside.'

Judd hesitated. He knew what McGreavy was leading up to. 'Yes.'

'Who had the keys to that lock?'

Judd felt his face reddening. 'Carol and I.'

McGreavy's voice was bland. 'What about the cleaning people? How did they get in?'

'We had a special arrangement with them. Carol came in early three mornings a week and let them in. They were finished before my first patient arrived.'

'That seems inconvenient. Why couldn't they get into these offices when they cleaned all the other offices?'

'Because the files I keep in here are of a highly confidential nature. I prefer the inconvenience to having strangers in here when no one is around.'

McGreavy looked over at the sergeant to make sure he was getting it all down. Satisfied, he turned back to Judd. 'When we walked into the reception office, the door was unlocked. Not forced – unlocked.'

Judd said nothing.

McGreavy went on. 'You just told us that the only ones who had a key to that lock were you and Carol. And we have Carol's key. Think again, Dr Stevens. Who else had a key to that door?'

'No one.'

'Then how do you suppose those men got in?'

And Judd suddenly knew. 'They made a copy of Carol's key when they killed her.'

'It's possible,' conceded McGreavy. A bleak smile touched his lips. 'If they made a copy, we'll find paraffin traces on her key. I'll have the lab run a test.'

Judd nodded. He felt as though he had scored a victory, but his feeling of satisfaction was short-lived.

'So the way you see it,' McGreavy said, 'two men – we'll assume for the moment there's no woman involved – had a key copied so they could get into your office and kill you. Right?'

'Right,' said Judd.

'Now you said that when you went into your office, you locked the inner door. True?'

'Yes,' Judd said.

McGreavy's voice was almost mild. 'But we found that door unlocked, too.'

'They must have had a key to it.'

'Then after they got it open, why didn't they kill you?'

'I told you. They heard the voices on the tape and – '

'These two desperate killers went to all the trouble to knock out the lights, trap you up here, break into your office – and then just vanished into thin air without harming a hair of your head?' His voice was filled with contempt.

Judd felt cold anger rising in him. 'What are you implying?'

'I'll spell it out for you, Doctor. I don't think anyone was here and I don't believe anyone tried to kill you.'

'You don't have to take my word for it,' Judd said angrily. 'What about the lights? What about the night watchman, Bigelow?'

'He's in the lobby.'

Judd's heart missed a beat. 'Dead?'

'He wasn't when he let us in. There was a faulty wire in the main power switch. Bigelow was down in the basement trying to fix it. He got it working just as I arrived.'

Judd looked at him numbly. 'Oh,' he said finally.

'I don't know what you're playing at, Dr Stevens,' McGreavy said, 'but from now on, count me out.' He moved towards the door. 'And do me a favour. Don't call me again – I'll call you.'

The sergeant snapped his notebook shut and followed McGreavy out.

The effects of the whisky had evaporated. The euphoria had gone, and he was left with a deep depression. He had no idea what his next move should be. He was on the inside of a puzzle that had no key. He felt like the boy who cried 'wolf', except that the wolves were deadly, unseen phantoms, and every time

McGreavy came, they seemed to vanish. Phantoms or . . . There was one other possibility. It was so horrifying that he couldn't bring himself to even acknowledge it. But he had to.

He had to face the possibility that he was a paranoiac.

A mind that was overstressed could give birth to delusions that seemed totally real. He had been working too hard. He had not had a vacation in years. It was conceivable that the deaths of Hanson and Carol could have been the catalyst that had sent his mind over some emotional precipice so that events became enormously magnified and out of joint. People suffering from paranoia lived in a land where everyday, commonplace things represented nameless terrors. Take the car accident. If it had been a deliberate attempt to kill him, surely the driver would have got out and made sure that the job was finished. And the two men who had come here tonight. He did not *know* that they had guns. Would a paranoiac not assume that they were there to kill him? It was more logical to believe that they were sneak thieves. When they had heard the voices in his inner office, they had fled. Surely, if they were assassins, they would have opened the unlocked door and killed him. How could he find out the truth? He knew it would be useless to appeal to the police again. There was no one to whom he could turn.

An idea began to form. It was born of desperation, but the more he examined it, the more sense it made. He picked up the telephone directory and began to riffle through the yellow pages.

Chapter Nine

At four o'clock the following afternoon Judd left his office and drove to an address on the lower West Side. It was an ancient, run-down brownstone apartment house. As he pulled up in front of the dilapidated building, Judd began to have misgivings. Perhaps he had the wrong address. Then a sign in a window of a first-floor apartment caught his eye:

NORMAN Z. MOODY
Private Investigator
SATISFACTION GUARANTEED

Judd alighted from the car. It was a raw, windy day with a forecast of late snow. He moved gingerly across the icy sidewalk and walked into the vestibule of the building.

The vestibule smelled of mingled odours of stale cooking and urine. He pressed the button marked 'Norman Z. Moody – 1', and a moment later a buzzer sounded. He stepped inside and found Apartment 1. A sign on the door read:

NORMAN Z. MOODY
Private Investigator
RING BELL AND ENTER

He rang the bell and entered.

Moody was obviously not a man given to throwing his money away on luxuries. The office looked as though it had been furnished by a blind, hyperthyroid pack rat. Odds and ends crammed every spare inch of the room. In one corner stood a tattered Japanese screen. Next to it was an East Indian lamp, and in front of the lamp a scarred Danish-modern table. Newspapers and old magazines were piled everywhere.

A door to an inner room burst open and Norman Z. Moody emerged. He was about five foot five and must have weighed three hundred pounds. He rolled as he walked, reminding Judd of an animated Buddha. He had a round, jovial face with wide, guileless, pale blue eyes. He was totally bald and his head was egg-shaped. It was impossible to guess his age.

'Mr Stevenson?' Moody greeted him.

'Dr Stevens,' Judd said.

'Sit down, sit down.' Buddha with a Southern drawl.

Judd looked around for a seat. He removed a pile of old body-building and nudist magazines from a scrofulous-looking leather armchair with strips torn out of it, and gingerly sat down.

Moody was lowering his bulk into an oversized rocking chair. 'Well, now! What can I do for you?'

Judd knew that he had made a mistake. Over the phone he had carefully given Moody his full name. A name that had been on the front page of every New York newspaper in the last few days. And he had managed to pick the only private detective in the whole city who had never even heard of him. He cast about for some excuse to walk out.

'Who recommended me?' Moody prodded.

Judd hesitated, not wanting to offend him. 'I got your name out of the yellow pages.'

Moody laughed. 'I don't know what I'd do without the yellow pages,' he said. 'Greatest invention since corn liquor.' He gave another little laugh.

Judd got to his feet. He was dealing with a total idiot. 'I'm sorry to have taken up your time, Mr Moody,' he said, 'I'd like to think about this some more before I . . .'

'Sure, sure. I understand,' Moody said. 'You'll have to pay me for the appointment, though.'

'Of course,' Judd said. He reached in his pocket and pulled out some bills. 'How much is it?'

'Fifty dollars.'

'Fifty – ?' Judd swallowed angrily, peeled off some bills and thrust them in Moody's hand. Moody counted the money carefully.

'Thanks a lot,' Moody said. Judd started towards the door, feeling like a fool. 'Doctor . . . '

Judd turned. Moody was smiling at him bene-volently, tucking the money into the pocket of his waistcoat. 'As long as you're stuck for the fifty dollars,' he said mildly, 'you might as well sit down and tell me what your problem is. I always say that nothin' takes more weight off than gettin' things off your chest.'

The irony of it, coming from this silly fat man, almost made Judd laugh. Judd's whole life was devoted to listening to people get things off their chests. He studied Moody a moment. What could he lose? Perhaps talking it out with a stranger would help. Slowly he went back to his chair and sat down.

'You look like you're carryin' the weight of the world, Doc. I always say that four shoulders are better than two.'

Judd was not certain how many of Moody's aphorisms he was going to be able to stand.

Moody was watching him. 'What brought you here? Women, or money? I always say if you took away women and money, you'd solve most of the world's problems right there.' Moody was eyeing him, waiting for an answer.

'I – I think someone is trying to kill me.'

Blue eyes blinked. 'You think?'

Judd brushed the question aside. 'Perhaps you could give me the name of someone who specializes in investigating that kind of thing.'

'I certainly can,' Moody said. 'Norman Z. Moody. Best in the country.'

Judd sighed in despair.

'Why don't you tell me about it, Doc?' Moody suggested. 'Let's see if the two of us can't sort it out a little.'

Judd had to smile in spite of himself. It sounded so much like himself. *Just lie down and say anything that comes into your mind.* Why not? He took a deep breath and, as concisely as possible, told Moody the events of the past few days. As he spoke, he forgot that Moody was there. He was really speaking to himself, putting into words the baffling things that had occurred. He carefully said nothing to Moody about his fears for his own sanity. When Judd had finished, Moody regarded him happily.

'You got yourself a dilly of a problem there. Either somebody's out to murder you, or you're afraid that you're becoming a schizophrenic paranoiac.'

Judd looked up in surprise. Score one for Norman Z. Moody.

Moody went on. 'You said there are two detectives on the case. Do you remember their names?'

Judd hesitated. He was reluctant to get too deeply committed to this man. All he really wanted to do was to get out of there. 'Frank Angeli,' he answered, 'and Lieutenant McGreavy.'

There was an almost imperceptible change in Moody's expression.

'What reason would anyone have to kill you, Doc?'

'I have no idea. As far as I know, I haven't any enemies.'

'Oh, come on. Everybody's got a few enemies layin' around. I always say enemies give a little salt to the bread of life.'

Judd tried not to wince.

'Married?'

'No,' Judd said.

'Are you a fairy?'

Judd sighed. 'Look, I've been through all this with the police and – '

'Yeah. Only you're payin' me to help you,' Moody said, unperturbed. 'Owe anybody any money?'

'Just the normal monthly bills.'

'What about your patients?'

'What about them?'

'Well, I always say if you're lookin' for seashells, go down to the seashore. Your patients are a lot of loonies. Right?'

'Wrong,' Judd said curtly. 'They're people with problems.'

'Emotional problems that they can't solve themselves. Could one of them have it in for you? Oh, not for any real reason, but maybe somebody with an imaginary grievance against you.'

'It's possible. Except for one thing. Most of my patients have been under my care for a year or more. In that length of time I've got to know them as well as one human being can know another.'

'Don't they never get mad at you?' Moody asked innocently.

'Sometimes. But we're not looking for someone who's angry. We're looking for a homicidal paranoiac who has murdered at least two people and has made several attempts to murder me.' He hesitated, then made himself go on. 'If I have a patient like that and don't know it, then you're looking at the most incompetent psychoanalyst who ever lived.'

He looked up and saw Moody studying him.

'I always say first things first,' Moody said cheerfully. 'The first thing we've gotta do is find out whether someone's trying to knock you off, or whether you're nuts. Right, Doc?' He broke into a broad smile, taking the offence out of his words.

'How?' Judd asked.

'Simple,' Moody said. 'Your problem is, you're standin' at home plate strikin' at curve balls, an' you don't know if anyone's pitchin'. First we gonna find out if there's a ball-game goin' on; then we're gonna find out who the players are. You got a car?'

'Yes.'

Judd had forgotten about walking out and finding another private detective. He sensed now behind

Moody's bland, innocent face and his homespun maxims a quiet, intelligent capability.

'I think your nerves are shot,' Moody said. 'I want you to take a little vacation.'

'When?'

'Tomorrow morning.'

'That's impossible.' Judd protested. 'I have patients scheduled . . .'

Moody brushed it aside. 'Cancel them.'

'But what good – '

'Do I tell you how to run your business?' Moody asked. 'When you leave here, I want you to go straight to a travel agency. Have them get you a reservation at' – he thought a moment – 'Grossinger's. That's a pretty drive up through the Catskills . . . Is there a garage in the apartment building where you live?'

'Yes.'

'Okay. Tell them to service your car for the trip. You don't want to have any breakdown on the road.'

'Couldn't I do this next week? Tomorrow is a full – '

'After you make your reservation, you're going back to your office and call all your patients. Tell them you've had an emergency and you'll be back in a week.'

'I really can't,' Judd said. 'It's out of the – '

'You'd better call Angeli, too,' Moody continued. 'I don't want the police hunting for you while you're gone.'

'Why am I doing this?' Judd asked.

'To protect your fifty dollars. That reminds me. I'm gonna need another two hundred for a retainer. Plus fifty a day for expenses.'

Moody hauled his large bulk up out of the big rocker.

'I want you to get a nice early start tomorrow,' he said, 'so you can get up there before dark. Can you leave about seven in the morning?'

'I . . . I suppose so. What will I find when I get up there?'

'With a little luck, a scorecard.'

Five minutes later Judd was thoughtfully getting into his car. He had told Moody that he could not go away and leave his patients on such short notice. But he knew that he was going to. He was literally putting his life into the hands of the Falstaff of the private detective world. As he started to drive away, his eye caught Moody's sign in the window.

SATISFACTION GUARANTEED.

He'd better be right, Judd thought grimly.

The plan for the trip went smoothly. Judd stopped at a travel agency on Madison Avenue. They reserved a room for him at Grossinger's and provided him with a road map and a variety of colour brochures on the Catskills. Next he telephoned his answering service and arranged for them to call his patients and cancel all his appointments until further notice. He phoned the Nineteenth Precinct and asked for Detective Angeli.

'Angeli's home sick,' said an impersonal voice. 'Do you want his home number?'

'Yes.'

A few moments later he was talking to Angeli. From the sound of Angeli's voice, he had a heavy cold.

'I've decided I need to get out of town for a few

days,' Judd said. 'I'm leaving in the morning. I wanted to check it with you.'

There was a silence while Angeli thought it over. 'It might not be a bad idea. Where will you go?'

'I thought I'd drive up to Grossinger's.'

'All right,' Angeli said. 'Don't worry. I'll clear it with McGreavy.' He hesitated. 'I heard what happened at your office last night.'

'You mean you heard McGreavy's version,' Judd said.

'Did you get a look at the men who tried to kill you?'

'No.'

'Nothing at all that could help us find them? Colour, age, height?'

'I'm sorry,' Judd said. 'It was dark.'

Angeli sniffed. 'Okay. I'll keep looking. Maybe I'll have some good news for you when you get back. Be careful, Doctor.'

'I will,' Judd said gratefully. And he hung up.

Next he phoned Harrison Burke's employer and briefly explained Burke's situation. There was no choice but to have him committed as soon as possible. Judd then called Peter, explained that he had to go out of town for a week, and asked him to make the necessary arrangements for Burke. Peter agreed.

The decks were clear.

The thing that disturbed Judd the most was that he would be unable to see Anne on Friday. Perhaps he would never see her again.

As he drove back towards his apartment, he thought about Norman Z. Moody. He had an idea what Moody was up to. By having Judd notify all his patients that he was going away, Moody was making sure that if one of Judd's patients was the killer – if there was a killer – a trap, using Judd as the bait, would be set for him.

Moody had instructed him to leave his forwarding address with his telephone exchange and with the doorman at the apartment building. He was making certain that everyone would know where Judd was going.

When Judd pulled up in front of the apartment house, Mike was there to greet him.

'I'm leaving on a trip in the morning, Mike,' Judd informed him. 'Will you make sure the garage services my car and fills the tank?'

'I'll have it taken care of, Dr Stevens. What time will you be needing the car?'

'I'll be leaving at seven.' Judd sensed Mike watching him as he walked into the apartment building.

When he entered his apartment, he locked the doors and carefully checked the windows. Everything seemed to be in order.

He took two codeine pills, got undressed, and ran a hot bath, gingerly easing his aching body into it, feeling the tensions soaking out of his back and neck. He lay in the blessedly relaxing tub, thinking. Why had Moody warned him not to let the car break down on the road? Because that was the most likely place for him to be attacked, somewhere on a lonely road in the Catskills? And what could Moody do about it if Judd were attacked? Moody had refused to tell him what his plan was – if there was a plan. The more Judd examined it, the more convinced he became that he was walking into a trap. Moody had said he was setting it up for Judd's pursuers. But no matter how many times he went over it, the answer always came out the same: the trap seemed designed to catch Judd. But why? What interest could Moody have in getting him killed? *My God*, thought Judd. *I've picked a name at random out of the yellow pages of the Manhattan Telephone Directory and I believe he wants to have me murdered! I am paranoiac!*

He felt his eyes beginning to close. The pills and the hot bath had done their work well. Wearily he pulled himself out of the tub, carefully patted his bruised body dry with a fluffy towel, and put on a pair of pyjamas. He got into bed and set the electric alarm clock for six. The Catskills, he thought. It was an appropriate name. And he fell into a deep, exhausted sleep.

At six a.m., when the alarm went off, Judd was instantly awake. As though there had been no time lapse at all, his first thought was, *I don't believe in a series of coincidences and I don't believe that one of my patients is a mass murderer*. Ergo, *I am either paranoiac, or am becoming one*. What he needed was to consult another psychoanalyst without delay. He would phone Dr Robbie. He knew that it would mean the end of his professional career, but there was no help for it. If he were suffering from paranoia, they would have to commit him. Did Moody suspect that he was dealing with a mental case? Was that why he suggested a vacation? Not because he believed anyone was after Judd's life, but because he could see the signs of a nervous breakdown? Perhaps the wisest course would be to follow Moody's advice and go to the Catskills for a few days. Alone, with all the pressures removed, he would calmly try to evaluate himself, try to reason out when his mind had started to trick him, when he had begun to lose touch with reality. Then, when he returned, he would make an appointment with Dr Robbie and put himself under his care.

It was a painful decision to make, but having made it, Judd felt better. He dressed, packed a small suitcase with enough clothes for five days, and carried it out to the elevator.

Eddie was not on duty yet, and the elevator was on self-service. Judd rode down to the basement garage. He looked round for Wilt, the attendant, but he was nowhere around. The garage was deserted.

Judd spotted his car parked in a corner against the cement wall. He walked over to it, put his suitcase in the back seat, opened the front door, and eased in behind the wheel. As he reached for the ignition key, a man loomed up at his side from nowhere. Judd's heart skipped a beat.

'You're right on schedule.' It was Moody.

'I didn't know you were going to see me off,' Judd said.

Moody beamed at him, his cherubic face breaking into a huge smile. 'I had nothing better to do and I couldn't sleep.'

Judd was suddenly grateful for the tactful way Moody had handled the situation. No reference to the fact that Judd was a mental case, just an ingenuous suggestion that he drive up to the country and take a rest. Well, the least Judd could do was to keep up the pretence that everything was normal.

'I decided you were right. I'm going to drive up and see if I can find a scorecard to the ballgame.'

'Oh, you don't have to go anywhere for that,' Moody said. 'That's all taken care of.'

Judd looked at him blankly. 'I don't understand.'

'It's simple. I always say when you want to get to the bottom of anything, you gotta start diggin'.'

'Mr Moody . . .'

Moody leaned against the door of the car. 'You know what I found intriguin' about your little problem, Doc? Seemed like every five minutes somebody was tryin' to kill you – maybe. Now that "maybe" fascinated me. There was nothin' for us to bite into till we found out whether you were crackin' up, or whether someone was really tryin' to turn you into a corpse.'

Judd looked at him. 'But the Catskills . . .' he said weakly.

'Oh, you wasn't never goin' to the Catskills, Doc.' He opened the door of the car. 'Step out here.'

Bewildered, Judd stepped out of the car.

'You see, that was just advertising. I always say if you wanta catch a shark, you've gotta bloody up the water first.'

Judd was watching his face.

'I'm afraid you never would have got to the Catskills,' Moody said gently. He walked around to the hood of the car, fumbled with the catch, and raised the hood. Judd walked over to his side. Taped to the distributor lead were three sticks of dynamite. Two thin wires were dangling loose from the ignition.

'Booby-trapped,' Moody said.

Judd looked at him, baffled. 'But how did you . . .'

Moody grinned at him. 'I told you, I'm a bad sleeper. I got here around midnight. I paid the nightman to go out and have some fun, an' I just kinda waited in the shadows. The nightman'll cost another twenty dollars,' he added. 'I didn't want you to look cheap.'

Judd felt a sudden wave of affection towards the little fat man. 'Did you see who did it?'

'Nope. It was done before I got here. At six o'clock this mornin' I figured no one was gonna show up any more, so I took a look.' He pointed to the dangling wires. 'Your friends are real cute. They rigged a second booby-trap so if you lifted the hood all the way, this wire would detonate the dynamite. The same thing would happen if you turned on your ignition. There's enough stuff here to wipe out half the garage.'

Judd felt suddenly sick to his stomach. Moody looked at him sympathetically. 'Cheer up,' he said. 'Look at the progress we've made. We know two things. First of all, we know you're not nuts. And secondly' – the smile left his face – 'we know that somebody is God Almighty anxious to murder you, Dr Stevens.'

Chapter Ten

They were sitting in the living-room of Judd's apart-ent, talking, Moody's enormous body spilling over the large couch. Moody had carefully put the pieces of the already defused bomb in the trunk of his own car.

'Shouldn't you have left it there so the police could have examined it?' Judd asked.

'I always say that the most confusin' thing in the world is too much information.'

'But it would prove to Lieutenant McGreavy that I've been telling the truth.'

'Would it?'

Judd saw his point. As far as McGreavy was concerned, Judd could have placed it there himself. Still, it seemed odd to him that a private detective would withhold evidence from the police. He had a feeling that Moody was like an enormous iceberg. Most of the man was concealed under the surface, under that façade of gentle, small-town bumbler. But now, as he listened to Moody talking, he was filled with elation. He was not insane and the world had not suddenly become filled with wild coincidences. There was an assassin on the loose. A flesh-and-blood assassin. And for some reason he had chosen Judd as his target. *My God*, thought Judd, *how easily our egos are destroyed*. A few minutes ago he had been ready to believe that he was paranoiac. He owed Moody an incalculable debt.

'. . . You're the doctor,' Moody was saying. 'I'm just an old gumshoe. I always say when you want honey, go to a beehive.'

Judd was beginning to understand Moody's jargon. 'You want my opinion about the kind of man, or men, we're looking for.'

'That's it,' beamed Moody. 'Are we dealin' with some homicidal maniac who broke out of a loony bin' –

Mental institution, Judd thought automatically.

– 'or have we got somethin' deeper goin' here?'

'Something deeper,' said Judd instantly.

'What makes you think so, Doc?'

'First of all, *two* men broke into my office last night. I might swallow the theory of one lunatic, but two lunatics working together is too much.'

Moody nodded approvingly. 'Gotcha. Go on.'

'Secondly, a deranged mind may have an obsession, but it works in a definite pattern. I don't know why John Hanson and Carol Roberts were killed, but unless I'm wrong, I'm scheduled to be the third and last victim.'

'What makes you think you're the last?' asked Moody curiously.

'Because,' replied Judd, 'if there were going to be other murders, then the first time they failed to kill me, they would have gone on to get whoever else was on their list. But instead of that, they've been concentrating on trying to kill me.'

'You know,' said Moody approvingly, 'you have the natural born makin's of a detective.'

Judd was frowning. 'There are several things that make no sense.'

'Such as?'

'First, the motive,' said Judd. 'I don't know anyone who – '

'We'll come back to that. What else?'

'If somebody really was that anxious to kill me, when the car knocked me down, all the driver had to do was to back up and run over me. I was unconscious.'

'Ah! That's where Mr Benson comes in.'

Judd looked at him blankly.

'Mr Benson is the witness to your accident,' explained Moody benevolently. 'I got his name from the police report and went to see him after you left my office. That'll be three-fifty for taxicabs. Okay?'

Judd nodded, speechless.

'Mr Benson – he's a furrier, by the way. Beautiful stuff. If you ever want to buy anything for your sweetheart, I can get you a discount. Anyway, Tuesday, the night of the accident, he was comin' out of an office building where his sister-in-law works. He dropped some pills off because his brother Matthew, who's a Bible salesman, had the flu an' she was goin' to take the pills home to him.'

Judd controlled his impatience. If Norman Z. Moody had felt like sitting there and reciting the entire Bill of Rights, he was going to listen.

'So Mr Benson dropped off these pills an' was comin' out of the building when he saw this limousine headin' towards you. Of course, he didn't know it was you at the time.'

Judd nodded.

'The car was kinda crabbin' sideways, an' from Benson's angle, it looked like it was in a skid. When he saw it hit you, he started runnin' over to see if he could help. The limousine backed up to make another run at you. He saw Mr Benson an' got out of there like a bat outta hell.'

Judd swallowed. 'So if Mr Benson hadn't happened along . . .'

'Yeah,' said Moody mildly. 'You might say you an' me wouldn't have met. These boys ain't playin' games. They're out to get you, Doc.'

'What about the attack in my office? Why didn't they break the door down?'

Moody was silent for a moment, thinking. 'That's a puzzler. They coulda broken in an' killed you an' whoever was with you an' got away without anybody seein' them. But when they thought you weren't alone, they left. It don't fit in with the rest.' He sat there worrying his lower lip. 'Unless . . .' he said.

'Unless what?'

A speculative look came over Moody's face. 'I wonder . . .' he breathed.

'What?'

'It'll keep for the time bein'. I got me a little idea, but it don't make sense until we find a motive.'

Judd shrugged helplessly. 'I don't know of anyone who has a motive for killing me.'

Moody thought about this a moment. 'Doc, could you have any secret that you shared with this patient of yours, Hanson, an' Carol Roberts? Somethin' maybe only the three of you knew about?'

Judd shook his head. 'The only secrets I have are professional secrets about my patients. And there's not one single thing in any of their case histories that would justify murder. None of my patients is a secret agent, or

115

a foreign spy, or an escaped convict. They're just ordinary people – housewives, professional men, bank clerks – who have problems they can't cope with.'

Moody looked at him guilelessly. 'An' you're sure that you're not harbouring a homicidal maniac in your little group?'

Judd's voice was firm. 'Positive. Yesterday I might not have been sure. To tell you the truth, I was beginning to think that I was suffering from paranoia and that you were humouring me.'

Moody smiled at him. 'The thought had crossed my mind,' he said. 'After you phoned me for an appointment, I did some checking up on you. I called a couple of pretty good doctor friends of mine. You got quite a reputation.'

So the 'Mr Stevenson' had been part of Moody's country bumpkin façade.

'If we go to the police now,' Judd said, 'with what we know, we can at least get them to start looking for whoever's behind all this.'

Moody looked at him in mild surprise. 'You think so? We don't really have much to go on yet, do we, Doc?'

It was true.

'I wouldn't be discouraged,' Moody said. 'I think we're makin' real progress. We've narrowed it down nicely.'

A note of frustration crept into Judd's voice. 'Sure. It could be anyone in the Continental United States.'

Moody sat there a moment, contemplating the ceiling. Finally he shook his head. 'Families,' he sighed.

'Families?'

'Doc – I believe you when you say you know your patients inside out. If you tell me they couldn't do anything like this, I have to go along with you. It's your beehive an' you're th' keeper of the honey.' He leaned forward on the couch. 'But tell me somethin'. When you take on a patient, do you interview his family?'

'No. Sometimes the family isn't even aware that the patient is undergoing psychoanalysis.'

Moody leaned back, satisfied. 'There you are,' he said.

Judd looked at him. 'You think that some member of a patient's family is trying to kill me?'

'Could be.'

'They'd have no more motive than the patient. Less, probably.'

Moody painfully pushed himself to his feet. 'You never know, do you. Doc? Tell you what I'd like you to do. Get me a list of all the patients you've seen in the last four or five weeks. Can you do that?'

Judd hesitated. 'No,' he said, finally.

'That confidential patient-doctor business? I think maybe it's time to bend that a little. Your life's at stake.'

'I think you're on the wrong track. What's been happening has nothing to do with my patients or their families. If there had been any insanity in their families, it would have come out in the psychoanalysis.' He shook his head. 'I'm sorry, Mr Moody. I have to protect my patients.'

'You said there was nothing in the files that was important.'

'Nothing that's important to us.' He thought of some

117

of the material in the files. John Hanson picking up sailors in gay bars on Third Avenue. Teri Washburn making love to the boys in the band. Fourteen-year-old Evelyn Warshak, the resident prostitute in the ninth grade . . . 'I'm sorry,' he said again. 'I can't show you the files.'

Moody shrugged. 'Okay,' he said. 'Okay. Then you're gonna have to do part of my job for me.'

'What do you want me to do?'

'Take out the tapes on everybody you've had on your couch for the last month. Listen real careful to each one. Only this time don't listen like a doctor – listen like a detective – look for anything the least bit offbeat.'

'I do that anyway. That's my job.'

'Do it again. An' keep your eyes open. I don't want to lose you till we solve this case.' He picked up his overcoat and struggled into it, making it look like an elephant ballet. Fat men were supposed to be graceful, thought Judd, but that did not include Mr Moody. 'Do you know the most peculiar thing about this whole megillah?' queried Moody thoughtfully.

'What?'

'You put your finger on it before, when you said there were *two* men. Maybe one man might have a burning itch to knock you off – but why *two*?'

'I don't know.'

Moody studied him a moment, speculatively. 'By God!' he finally said.

'What is it?'

'I just might have a brainstorm. If I'm right, there could be *more* than two men out to kill you.'

Judd stared at him incredulously. 'You mean there's

118

a whole group of maniacs after me? That doesn't make sense.'

There was a look of growing excitement on Moody's face. 'Doctor, I've got an idea who the umpire in this ball-game might be.' He looked at Judd, his eyes bright. 'I don't know how yet, or why – but it could be I know *who*.'

'Who?'

Moody shook his head. 'You'd have me sent to a cracker factory if I told you. I always say if you're gonna shoot off your mouth, make sure it's loaded first. Let me do a little target practice. If I'm on the right track, I'll tell you.'

'I hope you are,' Judd said earnestly.

Moody looked at him a moment. 'No, Doc. If you value your life worth a damn – pray I'm wrong.'

And Moody was gone.

He took a taxi to the office.

It was Friday noon, and with only three more shopping days until Christmas, the streets were crowded with late shoppers, bundled up against the raw wind sweeping in from the Hudson River. The store windows were festive and bright, filled with lighted Christmas trees and carved figures of the Nativity. Peace on Earth. Christmas. And Elizabeth, and their unborn baby. One day soon – if he survived – he would have to make his own peace, free himself from the dead past and let go. He knew that with Anne he could have . . . He firmly stopped himself. What was the point in fantasizing about a married woman about to go away with her husband, whom she loved?

The taxi pulled up in front of his office building and

Judd got out, nervously looking around. But what could he look for? He had no idea what the murder weapon would be, or who would wield it.

When he reached his office, he locked the outer door, went to the panelling that concealed the tapes, and opened it. The tapes were filed chronologically, under the name of each patient. He selected the most recent ones and carried them over to the tape recorder. With all his appointments cancelled for the day, he would be able to concentrate on trying to find some clue that might involve the friends or families of his patients. He felt that Moody's suggestion was far-fetched, but he had too much respect for him to ignore it.

As he put on the first tape, he remembered the last time he had used the machine. Was it only last night? The memory filled him again with the sharp sense of nightmare. Someone had planned to murder him here in this room, where they had murdered Carol.

He suddenly realized that he had given no thought to his patients at the free hospital clinic where he worked one morning a week. It was probably because the murders had revolved around this office rather than the hospital. Still . . . He walked over to the section of the cabinets labelled 'CLINIC', looked through some of the tapes, and finally selected half a dozen. He put the first one on the tape recorder.

Rose Graham.

'. . . an accident, Doctor. Nancy cries a lot. She's always been a whiny baby, so when I hit her, it's for her own good y'know?'

'Did you ever try to find out why Nancy cries a lot?' Judd's voice asked.

"Cause she's spoiled. Her daddy spoiled her rotten and then run off and left us. Nancy always thought she was daddy's girl, but how much could Harry really have loved her if he run off like that?'

'You and Harry were never married, were you?'

'Well . . . Common law, I guess you'd call it. We was goin' to get married.'

'How long did you live together?'

'Four years.'

'How long was it after Harry left you that you broke Nancy's arm?'

''Bout a week, I guess. I didn't mean to break it. It's just that she wouldn't stop whining, so I finally picked up this curtain rod an' started beating on her.'

'Do you think Harry loved Nancy more than he loved you?'

'No. Harry was crazy about me.'

'Then why do you think he left you?'

'Because he was a man. An' y'know what men are? Animals! All of you! You should all be slaughtered like pigs!' Sobbing.

Judd switched off the tape and thought about Rose Graham. She was a psychotic misanthrope, and she had nearly beaten her six-year-old child to death on two separate occasions. But the pattern of the murders did not fit Rose Graham's psychosis.

He put on the next tape from the clinic.

Alexander Fallon.

'The police say that you attacked Mr Champion with a knife, Mr Fallon.'

'I only did what I was told.'

'Someone told you to kill Mr Champion?'

'He told me to do it.'

121

'He?'

'God.'

'Why did God tell you to kill him?'

'Because Champion's an evil man. He's an actor. I saw him on the stage. He kissed this woman. This actress. In front of the whole audience. He kissed her and . . .'

Silence.

'Go on.'

'He touched her – her titty.'

'Did that upset you?'

'Of course! It upset me terribly. Don't you understand what that meant? He had carnal knowledge of her. When I came out of that theatre, I felt like I had just come from Sodom and Gomorrah. They had to be punished.'

'So you decided to kill him.'

'I didn't decide it. God decided. I just carried out His orders.'

'Does God often talk to you?'

'Only when there's His work to be done. He's chosen me as His instrument, because I'm pure. Do you know what makes me pure? Do you know what the most cleansing thing in the world is? Slaying the wicked!'

Alexander Fallon. Thirty-five, a part-time baker's assistant. He had been sent to a mental home for six months and then released. Could God have told him to destroy Hanson, a homosexual, and Carol, a former prostitute, and Judd, their benefactor? Judd decided that it was unlikely. Fallon's thought processes took place in brief, painful spasms. Whoever had planned the murders was highly organized.

He played several more of the tapes from the clinic,

but none of them fitted into the pattern he was searching for. No. It wasn't any patient at the clinic.

He looked over the office files again and a name caught his eye.

Skeet Gibson.

He put on the tape.

"Mornin', Dockie. How do you like this bee-u-ti-ful day I cooked up for you?'

'You're feeling good today.'

'If I was feelin' any better, they'd have me locked up. Did you catch my show last night?'

'No. I'm sorry, I wasn't able to.'

'I was only a smash. Jack Gould called me "the most lovable comedian in the world". An' who am I to argue with a genius like Jack Gould? You shoulda heard that audience! They were applauding like it was going out of style. Do ya know what that proves?'

'That they can read "Applause" cards?'

'You're sharp, you devil you. That's what I like – a head-shrinker with a sense of humour. The last one I had was a drag. Had a great big beard that really bugged me.'

'Why?'

'Because it was a lady!'

Loud laughter.

'Gotcha that time, didn't I, old cock? Seriously, folks, one of the reasons I'm feelin' so good is because I just pledged a million dollars – count 'em: one million bucks – to help the kids in Biafra.'

'No wonder you feel good.'

'You bet your sweet ass. That story hit the front pages all over the world.'

'Is that important?'

123

'What do you mean, "Is that important?" How many guys pledge that kind of loot? You've gotta blow your own horn, Peter Pan. I'm glad I can afford to pledge the money.'

'You keep saying "pledge". Do you mean "give"?'

'Pledge – give – what's the difference? You pledge a million – give a few grand – an' they kiss your ass . . . Did I tell you it's my anniversary today?'

'No. Congratulations.'

'Thanks. Fifteen great years. You never met Sally. There's the sweetest broad that ever walked God's earth. I really got lucky with my marriage. You know what a pain in the keester in-laws can be? Well, Sally's got these two brothers, Ben an' Charley. I told you about them. Ben's head writer on my TV show an' Charley's my producer. They're geniuses. I've been on the air seven years now. An' we're never outta the top ten in the Nielsen's. I was smart to marry into a family like that, huh? Most women get fat an' sloppy once they've hooked their husband. But Sally, bless her, is slimmer now than the day we were married. What a dame! . . . Got a cigarette?'

'Here. I thought you quit smoking.'

'I just wanted to show myself I had the old willpower, so I quit. Now I'm smoking because I want to . . . I made a new deal with the network yesterday. I really shafted 'em. Is my time up yet?'

'No. Are you restless, Skeet?'

'To tell you the truth, sweetie, I'm in such great shape I don't know what the hell I'm coming in here any more for.'

'No more problems?'

'Me? The world's my oyster an' I'm Diamond Jim

Brady. I've gotta hand it to you. You've really helped me. You're my man. With the kind of money you make, maybe I should go into business and set up my own shingle, huh? . . . That reminds me of the great story of the guy who goes to a wig-picker, but he's so nervous he just lays on the couch and doesn't say anything. At the end of the hour, the shrink says, "That'll be fifty dollars." Well, that goes on for two whole years without the schmuck saying one word. Finally the little guy opens his mouth one day and says, "Doctor – could I ask you a question?" "Sure," says the Doc. And the little guy says, "Would you like a partner?"'

Loud laughter.

'You got a shot of aspirin or somethin'?'

'Certainly. Is it one of your bad headaches?'

'Nothin' I can't handle, old buddy . . . Thanks. That'll do the trick.'

'What do you think brings these headaches on?'

'Just normal show-biz tension . . . We have our script reading this afternoon.'

'Does that make you nervous?'

'Me? Hell, no! What have I got to be nervous about? If the jokes are lousy, I make a face, wink at the audience, an' they eat it up. No matter how bad the show is, little old Skeet comes out smelling like a rose.'

'Why do you think you have these headaches every week?'

'How the fuck do I know? You're supposed to be a doctor. *You* tell *me*. I don't pay you to sit on your fat ass for an hour asking stupid questions. Jesus Christ, if an idiot like you can't cure a simple headache, they shouldn't let you be running around loose, messing up people's lives. Where'd you get your medical certificate? From a veterinarian school? I wouldn't trust my fuckin' cats with you. You're a goddamn quack! The only reason I came to you in the first place was because Sally shitted me into it. It was the only way I could get her off my back. Do ya know my definition of Hell? Bein' married to an ugly, skinny nag for fifteen years. If you're lookin' for some more suckers to cheat, take on her two idiot brothers, Ben an' Charley. Ben, my head writer, doesn't know which end of the pencil has the lead in it, an' his brother's even stupider. I wish they'd all drop dead. They're out to get me. You think I like you? You stink! You're so goddamn smug, sitting there looking down on everybody. You haven't got any problems, have you? Do you know why? Because you're not for real. You're out of it. All you do is sit on your fat keester all day long an' steal money from sick people. Well, I'm gonna get you, you sonofabitch. I'm gonna report you to the AMA . . .'

Sobbing.

'I wish I didn't have to go to that goddamn reading.'

Silence.

'Well – keep your pecker up. See ya next week, sweetie.'

Judd switched off the recorder. Skeet Gibson, America's most beloved comedian, should have been institutionalized ten years ago. His hobbies were beating up young, blonde showgirls and getting into bar-room brawls. Skeet was a small man, but he had started out as a prizefighter, and he knew how to hurt. One of his favourite sports was going into a gay bar, coaxing an unsuspecting homosexual into the men's room, and beating him unconscious. Skeet had been picked up by the police several times, but the incidents had always been hushed up. After all, he was America's most lovable comic. Skeet was paranoid enough to want to kill, and he was capable of killing in a fit of rage. But Judd did not think he was cold-blooded enough to carry out this kind of planned vendetta. And in that, Judd felt certain, lay the key to the solution. Whoever was trying to murder him was doing it not in the heat of any passion, but methodically and cold-bloodedly. A madman.

Who was not mad.

Chapter Eleven

The phone rang. It was his answering service. They had been able to reach all his patients except Anne Blake. Judd thanked the operator and hung up.

So Anne was coming here today. He was disturbed at how unreasonably happy he was at the thought of seeing her. He must remember that she was only coming by because he had asked her to, as her doctor. He sat there thinking about Anne. How much he knew her . . . and how little.

He put Anne's tape on the tape recorder and listened to it. It was one of her first visits.

'Comfortable, Mrs Blake?'

'Yes, thank you.'

'Relaxed?'

'Yes.'

'You're clenching your fists.'

'Perhaps I am a little tense.'

'About what?'

A long silence.

'Tell me about your home life. You've been married six months.'

'Yes.'

'Go on.'

'I'm married to a wonderful man. We live in a beautiful house.'

'What kind of house is it?'

'Country French . . . It's a lovely old place. There's a long, winding driveway leading to it. High up on the roof there's a funny old bronze rooster with its tail missing. I think some hunter shot it off a long time ago. We have about five acres, mostly wooded. I go for long walks. It's like living in the country.'

'Do you like the country?'

'Very much.'

'Does your husband?'

'I think so.'

'A man doesn't usually buy five acres in the country unless he loves it.'

'He loves me. He would have bought it for me. He's very generous.'

'Let's talk about him.'

Silence.

'Is he good-looking?'

'Anthony's very handsome.'

Judd felt a pang of unreasonable, unprofessional jealousy.

'You're compatible physically?' It was like a tongue probing at a sore tooth.

'Yes.'

He knew what she could be like in bed: exciting and feminine and giving. *Christ*, he thought, *get off the subject*.

'Do you want children?'

'Oh, yes.'

'Does your husband?'

'Yes, of course.'

A long silence except for the silky rustling of the tape. Then:

'Mrs Blake, you came to me because you said you

129

had a desperate problem. It concerns your husband, doesn't it?'

Silence.

'Well, I'm assuming it does. From what you told me earlier, you love each other, you're both faithful, you both want children, you live in a beautiful home, your husband is successful, handsome, and he spoils you. And you've only been married six months. I'm afraid it's a little like the old joke: "What's my problem, Doctor?"'

There was silence again except for the impersonal whirring of the tape. Finally she spoke. 'It's . . . it's difficult for me to talk about. I thought I could discuss it with a stranger, but' – he remembered vividly how she had twisted around on the couch to look up at him with those large, enigmatic eyes – 'it's harder. You see' – and she was speaking more rapidly now, trying to overcome the barriers that had kept her silent – 'I overheard something and I – I could easily have jumped to the wrong conclusion.'

'Something to do with your husband's personal life? Some woman?'

'No.'

'His business?'

'Yes . . .'

'You thought he lied about something? Tried to get the better of someone in a deal?'

'Something like that.'

Judd was on surer ground now. 'And it upset your confidence in him. It showed you a side of him that you had never seen before.'

'I – I can't discuss it. I feel disloyal to him even being

130

here. Please don't ask me anything more today, Dr Stevens.'

And that had ended that session. Judd switched off the tape.

So Anne's husband had pulled a sharp business deal. He could have cheated on his taxes. Or forced someone into bankruptcy. Anne, naturally, would be upset. She was a sensitive woman. Her faith in her husband would be shaken.

He thought about Anne's husband as a possible suspect. He was in the construction business. Judd had never met him, but whatever business problem he was involved in could not, by any stretch of the imagination, have included John Hanson, Carol Roberts, or Judd.

But what about Anne herself? Could she be a psychopath? A homicidal maniac? Judd leaned back in his chair and tried to think about her objectively.

He knew nothing about her except what she had told him. Her background could have been fictitious, she could have made it all up, but what would she have to gain? If this was some elaborate charade as a cover to murder, there had to be a motivation. The memory of her face and her voice flooded his mind, and he knew that she could have nothing to do with any of this. He would stake his life on it. The irony of the phrase made him grin.

He went over to get the tapes of Teri Washburn. Perhaps there was something there that he might have missed.

Teri had been having extra sessions lately at her own request. Was she under some new pressure that she had not yet confided to him? Because of her incessant preoccupation with sex, it was difficult to determine accurately her current progress. Still – why had she suddenly, urgently asked for more time with him?

Judd picked up one of her tapes at random and put it on.

'Let's talk about your marriages, Teri. You've been married five times.'

'Six, but who's counting?'

'Were you faithful to your husbands?'

Laughter.

'You're putting me on. There isn't a man in the world who can satisfy me. It's a physical thing.'

'What do you mean by "a physical thing"?'

'I mean that's the way I'm built. I just got a hot hole and it's gotta be kept filled all the time.'

'Do you believe that?'

'That it's gotta be kept filled?'

'That you're different, physically, from any other woman.'

'Certainly. The studio doctor told me. It's a glandular thing or something.' A pause. 'He was a lousy lay.'

'I've seen all your charts. Physiologically your body is normal in every respect.'

'Fuck the charts, Charley. Why don't you find out for yourself?'

'Have you ever been in love, Teri?'

'I could be in love with you.'

Silence.

'Get that look off your face. I can't help it. I told you. It's the way I'm built. I'm always hungry.'

'I believe you. But it's not your body that's hungry. It's your emotions.'

132

'I've never been fucked in my emotions. Do you want to give it a whirl?'

'No.'

'What do you want?'

'To help you.'

'Why don't you come over here and sit down next to me?'

'That will be all for today.'

Judd switched off the tape. He remembered a dialogue they had had when Teri was talking about her career as a big star and he had asked her why she had left Hollywood.

'I slapped some obnoxious jerk at a drunken party,' she had said. 'And he turned out to be Mr Big. He had me thrown out of Hollywood on my Polack ass.'

Judd had not probed any farther because at that time he was more interested in her home background, and the subject had never come up again. Now he felt a small nagging doubt. He should have explored it farther. He had never had any interest in Hollywood except in the way Dr Louis Leakey or Margaret Mead might be interested in the natives of Patagonia. Who would know about Teri Washburn, the glamour star?

Norah Hadley was a movie buff. Judd had seen a collection of movie magazines at their house and had kidded Peter about them. Norah had spent the entire evening defending Hollywood. He picked up the receiver and dialled.

Norah answered the phone.

'Hello,' said Judd.

'Judd!' Her voice was warm and friendly. 'You called to tell me when you're coming to dinner.'

'We'll do it soon.'

'You'd better,' she said. 'I promised Ingrid. She's beautiful.'

Judd was sure she was. But not in the way Anne was beautiful.

'You break another date with her and we'll be at war with Sweden.'

'It won't happen again.'

'Are you all over your accident?'

'Oh, yes.'

'What a horrible thing that was.'

There was a hesitant note in Norah's voice. 'Judd . . . about Christmas Day. Peter and I would like you to share it with us. Please.'

He felt the old familiar tightening in his chest. They went through this every year. Peter and Norah were his dearest friends, and they hated it that he spent every Christmas alone, walking among strangers, losing himself in alien crowds, driving his body to keep moving until he was too exhausted to think. It was as though he were celebrating some terrible black mass for the dead, letting his grief take possession of him and tear him apart, lacerating and shriving him in some ancient ritual over which he had no control. *You're dramatizing it,* he told himself wearily.

'Judd . . .'

He cleared his throat. 'I'm sorry, Norah.' He knew how much she cared. 'Perhaps next Christmas.'

She tried to keep the disappointment out of her voice. 'Sure. I'll tell Pete.'

'Thanks.' He suddenly remembered why he had called. 'Norah – do you know who Teri Washburn is?'

'*The* Teri Washburn? The star? Why do you ask?'

'I – I saw her on Madison Avenue this morning.'

'In person? Honestly?' She was like an eager child. 'How did she look? Old? Young? Thin? Fat?'

'She looked fine. She used to be a pretty big star, didn't she?'

'*Pretty* big? Teri Washburn was the *biggest* – and in every way, if you know what I mean.'

'Whatever made a girl like that leave Hollywood?'

'She didn't exactly leave. She was booted out.'

So Teri had told him the truth. Judd felt better.

'You doctors keep your heads buried in the sand, don't you? Teri Washburn was involved in one of the hottest scandals Hollywood ever had.'

'Really?' said Judd. 'What happened?'

'She murdered her boyfriend.'

Chapter Twelve

It had started to snow again. From the street fifteen floors below, the sounds of traffic floated up, muted by the white, cottony flakes in the arctic wind. In a lighted office across the street he saw the blurred face of a secretary streaming down the window.

'Norah – are you certain?'

'When it comes to Hollywood, you're talking to a walking encyclopaedia, love. Teri was living with the head of Continental Studios but she was keeping an assistant director on the side. She caught him cheating on her one night and she stabbed him to death. The head of the studio pulled a lot of strings and paid off a lot of people and it was hushed up and called an accident. Part of the arrangement was that she get out of Hollywood and never come back. And she never has.'

Judd stared at the phone numbly.

'Judd, are you there?'

'I'm here.'

'You sound funny.'

'Where did you hear all this?'

'Hear it? It was in all the newspapers and fan magazines. Everybody knew about it.'

Except him. 'Thanks, Norah,' he said. 'Say hello to Peter.' He hung up.

So that was the 'casual incident'. Teri Washburn had

murdered a man and had never mentioned it to him. And if she had murdered once . . .

Thoughtfully he picked up a pad and wrote down 'Teri Washburn.'

The phone rang. Judd picked it up. 'Dr Stevens . . .'

'Just checking to see if you're all right.' It was Detective Angeli. His voice was still hoarse with a cold.

A feeling of gratitude filled Judd. Someone was on his side.

'Anything new?'

Judd hesitated. He could see no point in keeping quiet about the bomb.

'They tried again.' Judd told Angeli about Moody and the bomb that had been planted in his car. 'That should convince McGreavy,' he concluded.

'Where's the bomb?' Angeli's voice was excited.

Judd hesitated. 'It's been dismantled.'

'It's been *what*?' Angeli asked incredulously. 'Who did that?'

'Moody. He didn't think it mattered.'

'*Didn't matter!* What does he think the Police Department is for? We might have been able to tell who planted that bomb just by looking at it. We keep a file of MOs.'

'MO?'

'*Modus operandi*. People fall into habit patterns. If they do something one way the first time, chances are they'll keep doing it the same – I don't have to tell *you*.'

'No,' said Judd thoughtfully. Surely Moody had known that. Had he some reason for not wanting to show the bomb to McGreavy?

'Dr Stevens – how did you hire Moody?'

'I found him in the yellow pages.' It sounded ridiculous even as he said it.

He could hear Angeli swallow. 'Oh. Then you really don't know a damn thing about him.'

'I know I trust him. Why?'

'Right now,' Angeli said, 'I don't think you should trust anybody.'

'But Moody couldn't possibly be connected with any of this. My God! I picked him out of the phone book at random.'

'I don't care where you got him. Something smells fishy. Moody says he set a trap to catch whoever's after you, but he doesn't close the trap until the bait's already been taken, so we can't pin it on anyone. Then he shows you a bomb in your car that he could have put there himself. And wins your confidence. Right?'

'I suppose you could look at it that way,' Judd said. 'But – '

'Maybe your friend Moody is on the level, and maybe he's setting you up. I want you to play it nice and cool until we find out.'

Moody *against* him? It was difficult to believe. And yet, he remembered his earlier doubts when he had thought Moody was sending him into an ambush.

'What do you want me to do?' asked Judd.

'How would you feel about leaving town? I mean *really* leaving town.'

'I can't leave my patients.'

'Dr Stevens – '

'Besides,' Judd added, 'it really wouldn't solve anything, would it? I wouldn't even know what I'm running away from. When I came back, it would just start all over again.'

There was a moment's silence. 'You have a point.' Angeli gave a sigh, and it turned into a wheeze. He sounded terrible. 'When do you expect to hear from Moody again?'

'I don't know. He thinks he has some idea of who's behind all this.'

'Has it occurred to you that whoever's behind this can pay Moody a lot more than you can?' There was an urgency in Angeli's voice. 'If he asks you to meet him, call me. I'll be home in bed for the next day or two. Whatever you do, Doctor, don't meet him alone!'

'You're building up a case out of nothing,' countered Judd. 'Just because Moody removed the bomb from my car –'

'There's more to it than that,' said Angeli. 'I have a hunch you picked the wrong man.'

'I'll call you if I hear from him,' promised Judd. He hung up, shaken. Was Angeli being overly suspicious? It was true that Moody could have been lying about the bomb in order to win Judd's confidence. Then the next step would be easy. All he would have to do would be to call Judd and ask him to meet him in some deserted place on the pretext of having some evidence for him. Then . . . Judd shuddered. Could he have been wrong about Moody's character? He remembered his reaction when he had first met Moody. He had thought that the man was ineffectual and not very bright. Then he realized that his homespun cover was a façade that concealed a quick, sharp brain. But that didn't mean that Moody could be trusted. And yet . . . He heard someone at the outer reception door and looked at his watch. *Anne!* He quickly locked the tapes away, walked over to the private corridor door, and opened it.

Anne was standing in the corridor. She was wearing a smartly tailored navy blue suit and a small hat that framed her face. She was dreamily lost in thought, unaware that Judd was watching her. He studied her, filling himself with her beauty, trying to find some imperfection, some reason for him to tell himself that she would be wrong for him, that he would one day find someone else better suited to him. The fox and the grapes. Freud was not the father of psychiatry. Aesop was.

'Hello,' he said.

She looked up, startled for an instant. Then she smiled. 'Hello.'

'Come in, Mrs Blake.'

She moved past him into the office, her firm body brushing his. She turned and looked at him with those incredible violet eyes. 'Did they find the hit-and-run driver?' There was concern on her face, a worried, genuine interest.

He felt again the insane urge to tell her everything. But he knew he could not. At best, it would be a cheap trick to win her sympathy. At worst, it might involve her in some unknown danger.

'Not yet.' He indicated a chair.

Anne was watching his face. 'You look tired. Should you be back at work so soon?'

Oh, God. He didn't think he could stand any sympathy. Not just now. And not from her. He said, 'I'm fine. I cancelled my appointments for today. My exchange wasn't able to reach you.'

An anxious expression crossed her face. She was

140

afraid she was intruding. Anne – intruding. 'I'm so sorry. If you'd rather I left . . .'

'Please, no,' he said quickly. 'I'm glad they couldn't reach you.' This would be the last time he saw her. 'How are you feeling?' he asked.

She hesitated, started to say something, then changed her mind. 'A little confused.'

She was looking at him oddly, and there was something in her look that touched a faint, long-lost chord that he could almost, but not quite, remember. He felt a warmth, flowing from her, an overpowering physical longing – and he suddenly realized what he was doing. He was attributing his own emotions to her. And for an instant he had been fooled, like any first-year psychiatry student.

'When do you leave for Europe?' he asked.

'On Christmas morning.'

'Just you and your husband?' He felt like a gibbering idiot, reduced to banalities. Babbitt, on an off day.

'Where will you go?'

'Stockholm – Paris – London – Rome.'

I'd love to show you Rome, thought Judd. He had spent a year there interning at the American hospital. There was a fantastic old restaurant called Cybèle near the Tivoli Gardens, high on a mountaintop by an ancient pagan shrine, where you could sit in the sun and watch the hundreds of wild pigeons darken the sky over the dappled cliffs.

And Anne was on her way to Rome with her husband.

'It will be a second honeymoon,' she said. There was strain in her voice, so faint that he might almost have imagined it. An untrained ear would not have caught it.

Judd looked at her more closely. On the surface she seemed calm, normal, but underneath he sensed a tension. If this was the picture of a young girl in love going to Europe on a second honeymoon, then a piece of the picture was missing.

And he suddenly realized what it was.

There was no excitement in Anne. Or if there was, it was overshadowed by a patina of some stronger emotion. Sadness? Regret?

He realized that he was staring at her. 'How – how long will you be away?' Babbitt strikes again.

A small smile crossed her lips, as though she knew what he was doing. 'I'm not certain,' she answered gravely. 'Anthony's plans are indefinite.'

'I see.' He looked down at the rug, miserable. He had to put an end to this. He couldn't let Anne leave, feeling that he was a complete fool. Send her away now. 'Mrs Blake . . .' he began.

'Yes?'

He tried to keep his voice light. 'I really got you back here under false pretences. It wasn't necessary for you to see me again. I just wanted to – to say goodbye.'

Oddly, puzzlingly, some of the tension seemed to drain out of her. 'I know,' she said quietly. 'I wanted to say goodbye, too.' There was something in her voice that caught at him again.

She was getting to her feet. 'Judd . . .' She looked up at him, holding his eyes with hers, and he saw in her eyes what she must have seen in his. It was a mirrored reflection of a current so strong that it was almost physical. He started to move towards her, then stopped. He could not let her become involved in the danger that surrounded him.

When he finally spoke, his voice was almost under control. 'Drop me a card from Rome.'

She looked at him for a long moment. 'Please take care of yourself, Judd.'

He nodded, not trusting himself to speak.

And she was gone.

The phone rang three times before Judd heard it. He picked it up.

'That you, Doc?' It was Moody. His voice practically leaped out of the telephone, crackling with excitement. 'You alone?'

'Yes.'

There was an odd quality in Moody's excitement that Judd could not quite identify. Caution? Fear?

'Doc – remember I told you I had a hunch who might be behind this?'

'Yes . . .'

'I was right.'

Judd felt a quick chill go through him. 'You know who killed Hanson and Carol?'

'Yeah. I know who. And I know why. You're next, Doctor.'

'Tell me – '

'Not over the phone,' said Moody. 'We'd better meet somewhere and talk about it. Come alone.'

Judd stared at the phone in his hand.

COME ALONE!

'Are you listening?' asked Moody's voice.

'Yes,' said Judd quickly. What had Angeli said? *Whatever you do, Doctor, don't meet him alone.* 'Why can't we meet here?' he asked, stalling for time.

143

'I think I'm being followed. I managed to shake them off. I'm calling from the Five Star Meat Packing Company. It's on Twenty-third Street, west of Tenth Avenue, near the docks.'

Judd still found it impossible to believe that Moody was setting a trap for him. He decided to test him. 'I'll bring Angeli.'

Moody's voice was sharp. 'Don't bring anyone. Come by yourself.'

And there it was.

Judd thought of the fat little Buddha at the other end of the phone. His guileless friend who was charging him fifty dollars a day and expenses to set him up for his own murder.

Judd kept his voice controlled. 'Very well,' he said. 'I'll be right over.' He tried one parting shot. 'Are you sure you really know who's behind this, Moody?'

'Dead sure, Doc. Have you ever heard of Don Vinton?' And Moody hung up.

Judd stood there, trying to sort out the storm of emotions that raced through him. He looked up Angeli's home number and dialled it. It rang five times, and Judd was filled with a sudden panicky fear that Angeli might not be at home. Dare he go meet Moody alone?

Then he heard Angeli's nasal voice. 'Hello.'

'Judd Stevens. Moody just called.'

There was a quickening in Angeli's voice. 'What did he say?'

Judd hesitated, feeling a last vestige of unreasonable loyalty and – yes, affection – towards the bumbling little fat man who was plotting to cold-bloodedly murder him. 'He asked me to meet him at the Five Star

Meat Packing Company. It's on Twenty-third Street near Tenth Avenue. He told me to come alone.'

Angeli laughed mirthlessly. 'I'll bet he did. Don't budge out of that office, Doctor. I'm going to call Lieutenant McGreavy. We'll both pick you up.'

'Right,' said Judd. He hung up slowly. Norman Z. Moody. The jolly Buddha from the yellow pages. Judd felt a sudden, inexplicable sadness. He had liked Moody. And trusted him.

And Moody was waiting to kill him.

Chapter Thirteen

Twenty minutes later Judd unlocked his office door to admit Angeli and Lieutenant McGreavy. Angeli's eyes were red and teary. His voice was hoarse. Judd had a momentary pang at having dragged him out of a sick-bed. McGreavy's greeting was a curt, unfriendly nod.

'I told Lieutenant McGreavy about the phone call from Norman Moody,' Angeli said.

'Yeah. Let's find out what the hell this is all about,' McGreavy said sourly.

Five minutes later they were in an unmarked police car speeding downtown on the West Side. Angeli was at the wheel. The light snowfall had stopped and the gruel-thin rays of the late afternoon sun had surrendered to the oppressive cover of storm clouds sweeping across the Manhattan sky. There was a loud clap of thunder in the distance and then a bright, jagged sword of lightning. Drops of rain began to spatter the windscreen. As the car continued downtown, tall, soaring skycrapers gave way to small, grimy tenements huddled together as if for comfort against the biting cold.

The car turned into Twenty-third Street, going west towards the Hudson River. They moved into a land of junk-yards and fix-it shops and dingy bars, then past that to blocks of garages, trucking yards and freight companies. As the car neared the corner of Tenth Avenue, McGreavy directed Angeli to pull over to the kerb.

'We'll get out here.' McGreavy turned to Judd. 'Did Moody say whether anyone would be with him?'

'No.'

McGreavy unbuttoned his overcoat and transferred his service revolver from his holster to his overcoat pocket. Angeli followed suit. 'Stay in back of us,' McGreavy ordered Judd.

The three men started walking, ducking their heads against the wind-lashed rain. Halfway down the block, they came to a dilapidated-looking building with a faded sign above the door that read:

FIVE STAR MEAT PACKING COMPANY

There were no cars or trucks or lights, no sign of life.

The two detectives walked up to the door, one on either side. McGreavy tested the door. It was locked. He looked around, but could see no bell. They listened. Silence, except for the sound of the rain.

'It looks closed,' Angeli said.

'It probably is,' McGreavy replied. 'The Friday before Christmas – most companies are knocking off at noon.'

'There must be a loading entrance.'

Judd followed the two detectives as they moved cautiously towards the end of the building, trying to avoid the puddles in their path. They came to a service alley, and looking down it, they could discern a loading platform with deserted trucks pulled up in front of it.

There was no activity. They moved forward until they reached the platform.

'Okay,' McGreavy said to Judd. 'Sing out.'

Judd hesitated, feeling unreasonably sad that he was betraying Moody. Then he lifted his voice. 'Moody!' The only response was the yowling of an angry tomcat disturbed in his search for dry shelter. 'Mr Moody!'

There was a large wooden sliding door on top of the platform, used to move the deliveries from inside the warehouse to the area where the trucks were loaded. There were no steps leading onto the platform. McGreavy hoisted himself up, moving with surprising agility for such a large man. Angeli followed, then Judd. Angeli walked over to the sliding door and pushed against it. It was unlocked. The great door rolled open with a loud, high-pitched scream of protest. The tomcat answered hopefully, forgetting about shelter. Inside the warehouse it was pitch black.

'Did you bring a flashlight?' McGreavy asked Angeli.

'No.'

'Shit!'

Cautiously they inched their way into the gloom. Judd called out again. 'Mr Moody! It's Judd Stevens.'

There was no sound except for the creaking of the boards as the men moved across the room. McGreavy rummaged in his pockets and pulled out a book of matches. He lit one and held it up. Its feeble, sputtering light cast a wavering yellow glow in what seemed to be an enormous empty cavern. The match guttered out. 'Find the goddamn light switch,' McGreavy said. 'That was my last match.'

Judd could hear Angeli groping along the walls looking for the light switch. Judd kept moving forward.

He could not see the other two men. 'Moody!' he called.

He heard Angeli's voice from across the room. 'Here's a switch.' There was a click. Nothing happened.

'The master switch must be off,' McGreavy said.

Judd bumped against a wall. As he put his hands out to brace himself, his fingers closed over a doorlatch. He shoved the latch up and pulled. A massive door swung open and a blast of frigid air hit him. 'I've found a door,' he called out. He stepped over a sill and cautiously moved forward. He heard the door close behind him and his heart began to hammer. Impossibly, it was darker here than in the other room, as though he had stepped into a deeper blackness.

'Moody! Moody . . .'

A thick, heavy silence. Moody *had* to be here somewhere. If he weren't, Judd knew what McGreavy would think. It would be the boy who cried wolf again.

Judd took another step forward and suddenly felt cold flesh lick against his face. He jerked away in panic, feeling the short hairs on his neck rise. He became aware of the strong smell of blood and death surrounding him. There was an evil in the darkness around him, waiting to close in on him. His scalp tingled with fear and his heart was beating so rapidly that it was difficult to breathe. With trembling fingers he fumbled for a book of matches in his overcoat, found one, and scraped a match against the cover. In its light he saw a huge dead eye loom up in front of his face, and it took a shocked second before he realized that he was looking at a slaughtered cow dangling from a meat hook. He had one brief glimpse of other animal carcasses hanging from hooks and the outline of a door in the far corner, before the match went out. The door probably led to an office. Moody could be in there, waiting for him.

Judd moved farther into the interior of the inky black cavern towards the door. He felt the cold brush of dead animal flesh again. He quickly stepped away and kept walking cautiously towards the office door. 'Moody!'

He wondered what was detaining Angeli and McGreavy. He moved past the slaughtered animals, feeling as though someone with a macabre sense of humour was playing a horrible maniacal joke. But who and why were beyond his imagining. As he neared the door, he collided with another hanging carcass.

Judd stopped to get his bearings. He lit his last remaining match. In front of him, impaled on a meat hook and grinning obscenely, was the body of Norman Z. Moody. The match went out,

Chapter Fourteen

The coroner's men had finished their work and gone. Moody's body had been taken away and everyone had departed except Judd, McGreavy, and Angeli. They were sitting in the manager's small office, decorated with several impressive calendar nudes, an old desk, a swivel chair, and two filing cabinets. The lights were on and an electric heater was going.

The manager of the plant, a Mr Paul Moretti, had been tracked down and pulled away from a pre-Christmas party to answer some questions. He had explained that since it was a holiday weekend, he had let his employees off at noon. He had locked up at twelve-thirty, and to the best of his knowledge, there had been no one on the premises at that time. Mr Moretti was belligerently drunk, and when McGreavy saw that he was going to be no further help, he had him driven home. Judd was barely conscious of what was happening in the room. His thoughts were on Moody, how cheerful and how full of life he had been, and how cruelly he had died. And Judd blamed himself. If he had not involved Moody, the little detective would be alive today.

It was almost midnight. Judd had wearily reiterated the story of Moody's phone call for the tenth time. McGreavy, hunched up in his overcoat, sat there watching him, chewing savagely on a cigar. Finally he spoke. 'Do you read detective stories?'

Judd looked at him, surprised. 'No, why?'

'I'll tell you why. I think you're just too goddamn good to be true, Dr Stevens. From the very beginning I've thought that you were in this thing up to your neck. And I told you so. So what happens? Suddenly you turn into the target instead of the killer. First you claim a car ran you down and – '

'A car *did* run him down,' Angeli reminded him.

'A rookie could answer that one,' McGreavy snapped. 'It could have been arranged by someone who's in this with the doctor.' He turned back to Judd. 'Next, you call Detective Angeli with a wild-eyed yarn about two men breaking into your office and trying to kill you.'

'They *did* break in,' said Judd.

'No, they didn't,' snapped McGreavy. 'They used a special key.' His voice hardened. 'You said there were only two of those keys to that office – yours and Carol Roberts's.'

'That's right. I told you – they copied Carol's key.'

'I know what you told me. I had a paraffin test run. Carol's key was never copied, Doctor.' He paused to let it sink in. 'And since I have her key – that leaves yours, doesn't it?'

Judd looked at him, speechless.

'When I didn't buy the loose maniac theory, you hire a detective out of the yellow pages and he conveniently finds a bomb planted in your car. Only I can't see it because it's not there any more. Then you decide it's time to throw me another body, so you go through that rigmarole with Angeli about a phone call to meet Moody, who knows this mysterious nut who's out to kill you. But guess what? We get here and find him hanging on a meat hook.'

Judd flushed angrily. 'I'm not responsible for what happened.'

McGreavy gave him a long, hard look. 'Do you know the only reason you're not under arrest? Because I haven't found any motive to this Chinese puzzle yet. But I will, Doctor. That's a promise.' He got to his feet.

Judd suddenly remembered. 'Wait a minute!' he said. 'What about Don Vinton?'

'What about him?'

'Moody said he was the man behind all this.'

'Do you know anyone named Don Vinton?'

'No,' Judd said. ' – I assumed he'd be known by the police.'

'I never heard of him.' McGreavy turned to Angeli. Angeli shook his head.

'Okay. Send out a make on Don Vinton. FBI. Interpol. Police chiefs in all major American cities.' He looked at Judd. 'Satisfied?'

Judd nodded. Whoever was behind all this must have some kind of criminal record. It should not be difficult to identify him.

He thought again of Moody, with his homely aphorisms and his quick mind. He must have been followed here. It was unlikely that he would have told anyone else about the rendezvous, because he had stressed the need for secrecy. At least they now knew the name of the man they were looking for.

Praemonitus, praemunitas.

Forewarned, forearmed.

The murder of Norman Z. Moody was splashed all over the front pages of the newspapers the next morning.

Judd picked up a paper on his way to the office. He was briefly mentioned as being a witness who had come across the body with the police, but McGreavy had managed to keep the full story out of the papers. McGreavy was playing his cards close to his chest. Judd wondered what Anne would think.

This was Saturday, when Judd made his morning rounds at the clinic. He had arranged for someone else to fill in for him there. He went to his office, travelling alone in the elevator and making sure that no one was lurking in the corridor. He wondered, even as he did so, how long anyone could live like this, expecting an assassin to strike at any moment.

Half a dozen times during the morning he started to pick up the phone and call Detective Angeli to ask about Don Vinton, but each time he controlled his impatience. Angeli would surely call him as soon as he knew something. Judd puzzled over what Don Vinton's motivation could be. He could have been a patient whom Judd had treated years ago, perhaps when he was an intern. Someone who felt that Judd had slighted him or injured him in some way. But he could remember no patient named Vinton.

At noon he heard someone try to open the corridor door to the reception room. It was Angeli. Judd could tell nothing from his expression except that he looked even more drawn and haggard. His nose was red, and he was sniffling. He walked into the inner office and wearily flopped into a chair.

'Have you got any answers yet on Don Vinton?' Judd asked eagerly.

Angeli nodded. 'We got back teletypes from the FBI, the police chiefs and every big city in the United States, and Interpol.' Judd waited, afraid to breathe. 'None of them ever heard of Don Vinton.'

Judd looked at Angeli incredulously, a sudden sinking sensation in his stomach. 'But that's impossible! I mean – *someone* must know him. A man who could do all this just didn't come out of nowhere!'

'That's what McGreavy said,' replied Angeli wearily. 'Doctor, my men and I spent the night checking out every Don Vinton in Manhattan and all the other boroughs. We even covered New Jersey and Connecticut.' He took a ruled sheet of paper out of his pocket and showed it to Judd. 'We found eleven Don Vintons in the phone book who spell their name "ton" – four who spell it "ten" – and two who spell it "tin". We even tried it as one name. We narrowed it down to five possibles and checked out every one of them. One is a paralytic. One of them is a priest. One is first vice-president of a bank. One of them is a fireman who was on duty when two of the murders occurred. It just left the last one. He runs a pet shop and he must be damn near eighty years old.'

Judd's throat was dry. He was suddenly aware of how much he had counted on this. Surely Moody wouldn't have given him the name unless he was certain. And he hadn't said that Don Vinton was an accomplice; he had said he was behind the whole thing. It was inconceivable that the police would have no record of a man like that. Moody had been murdered because he had got onto the truth. And now that Moody was out of the way, Judd was completely alone. The web was drawing tighter.

'I'm sorry,' Angeli said.

Judd looked at the detective and suddenly remembered that Angeli had not been home all night. 'I appreciate your trying,' he said gratefully.

Angeli leaned forward. 'Are you positive you heard Moody right?'

'Yes.' Judd closed his eyes in concentration. He had asked Moody if he was sure who was really behind this. He heard Moody's voice again. *Dead sure. Have you ever heard of Don Vinton? Don Vinton.* He opened his eyes. 'Yes,' he repeated.

Angeli sighed. 'Then we're at a dead end.' He laughed mirthlessly. 'No pun intended.' He sneezed.

'You'd better get to bed.'

Angeli stood up. 'Yeah. I guess so.'

Judd hesitated. 'How long have you been McGreavy's partner?'

'This is our first case together. Why?'

'Do you think he's capable of framing me for murder?'

Angeli sneezed again. 'I think maybe you're right, Doctor. I'd better get to bed.' He walked over to the door.

'I may have a lead,' Judd said.

Angeli stopped and turned. 'Go on.'

Judd told him about Teri. He added that he was also going to check out some of John Hanson's former boyfriends.

'It doesn't sound like much,' Angeli said frankly. 'But I guess it's better than nothing.'

'I'm sick and tired of being a target. I'm going to start fighting back. I'm going after them.'

Angeli looked at him. 'With what? We're fighting shadows.'

'When witnesses describe a suspect, the police have

156

an artist draw up a composite picture of all the descriptions. Right?'

Angeli nodded. 'An identikit.'

Judd began to pace in restless excitement. 'I'm going to give you an identikit of the personality of the man who's behind this.'

'How can you? You've never seen him. It could be anyone.'

'No it couldn't,' Judd corrected. 'We're looking for someone very, very special.'

'Someone who's insane.'

'Insanity is a catchall phrase. It has no medical meaning. Sanity is simply the ability of the mind to adjust to reality. If we can't adjust, we either hide from reality, or we put ourselves above life, where we're super-beings who don't have to follow the rules.'

'Our man thinks he's a super-being.'

'Exactly. In a dangerous situation we have three choices, Angeli. Flight, constructive compromise, or attack. Our man attacks.'

'So he's a lunatic.'

'No. Lunatics rarely kill. Their concentration span is extremely short. We're dealing with someone more complicated. He could be somatic, hypophrenic, schizoid, cycloid – or any combination of these. We could be dealing with a fugue – temporary amnesia preceded by irrational acts. But the point is, his appearance and behaviour will seem perfectly normal to everyone.'

'So we have nothing to go on.'

'You're wrong. We have a good deal to go on. I can give you a physical description of him,' said Judd. He narrowed his eyes, concentrating. 'Don Vinton is above average height, well proportioned, and has the build of an athlete. He's neat in his appearance and meticulous about everything he does. He has no artistic talent. He doesn't paint or write or play the piano.'

Angela was staring at him, open-mouthed.

Judd continued, speaking more quickly now, warming up. 'He doesn't belong to any social clubs or organizations. Not unless he runs them. He's a man who has to be in charge. He's ruthless, and he's impatient. He thinks big. For example, he'd never get involved in petty thefts. If he had a record, it would be for bank robbery, kidnapping, or murder.' Judd's excitement was growing. The picture was growing sharper in his mind. 'When you catch him, you'll find that he was probably rejected by one of his parents when he was a boy.'

Angeli interrupted. 'Doctor, I don't want to shoot down your balloon, but it could be some crazy, hopped-up junkie who – '

'No. The man we're looking for doesn't take drugs.' Judd's voice was positive. 'I'll tell you something else about him. He played contact sports in school. Football or hockey. He has no interest in chess, word games, or puzzles.'

Angeli was watching him sceptically. 'There was more than one man,' he objected. 'You said so yourself.'

'I'm giving you a description of Don Vinton,' said Judd. 'The man who's masterminding this. I'll tell you something more about him. He's a Latin type.'

'What makes you think so?'

'Because of the methods used in the murders. A knife – acid – a bomb. He's South American, Italian, or

158

Spanish.' He took a breath. 'There's your identikit. That's the man who's committed three murders and is trying to kill me.'

Angeli swallowed. 'How the hell do you know all this?'

Judd sat down and leaned towards Angeli. 'It's my profession.'

'The mental side, sure. But how can you give a physical description of a man you've never seen?'

'I'm playing the odds. A doctor named Kretschmer found that eighty-five per cent of people suffering from paranoia have well-built, athletic bodies. Our man is an obvious paranoiac. He has delusions of grandeur. He's a megalomaniac who thinks he's above the law.'

'Then why wasn't he locked up a long time ago?'

'Because he's wearing a mask.'

'He's what?'

'We all wear masks, Angeli. From the time we're past infancy, we're taught to conceal our real feelings, to cover up our hatreds and fears.' There was authority in his voice. 'But under stress, Don Vinton is going to drop his mask and show his naked face.'

'I see.'

'His ego is his vulnerable point. If it's threatened – really threatened – he'll crack. He's on the thin edge now. It won't take much to send him completely over.' He hesitated, then went on, speaking almost to himself. 'He's a man with – mana.'

'With what?'

'Mana. It's a term that the primitives use for a man who exerts influence on others because of the demons in him, a man with an overpowering personality.'

159

'You said he doesn't paint, write, or play the piano. How do you know that?'

'The world is full of artists who are schizoids. Most of them manage to get through life without any violence because their work gives them an outlet in which to express themselves. Our man doesn't have that outlet. So he's like a volcano. The only way he can get rid of the pressure inside him is to erupt: Hanson – Carol – Moody.'

'You mean these were just senseless crimes that he committed to – '

'Not senseless to him. On the contrary . . .' His mind raced ahead swiftly. Several more pieces of the puzzle were beginning to fall into place. He cursed himself for having been too blind, or frightened, to see them. 'I'm the only one Don Vinton has been after – the prime target. John Hanson was killed because he was mistaken for me. When the killer found out his mistake, he came to the office for another try. I had gone, but he found Carol there.' His voice was angry.

'He killed her so she couldn't identify him?'

'No. The man we're looking for isn't a sadist. Carol was tortured because he wanted something. Say, a piece of incriminating evidence. And she wouldn't – or couldn't – give it to him.'

'What kind of evidence?' probed Angeli.

'I have no idea,' Judd said. 'But it's the key to this whole thing. Moody found out the answer, and that's why they killed him.'

'There's one thing that still doesn't make sense. If they had killed you on the street, then they couldn't have got the evidence. It doesn't fit with the rest of your theory,' Angeli persisted.

'It could. Let's assume that the evidence is on one of my tapes. It might be perfectly harmless by itself, but if I put it together with other facts, it could threaten them. So they have two choices. Either take it away from me, or eliminate me so I can't reveal it to anyone. First they tried to eliminate me. But they made a mistake and killed Hanson. Then they went to the second alternative. They tried to get it from Carol. When that failed, they decided to concentrate on killing me. That was the car accident. I was probably followed when I went to hire Moody, and he, in turn, was followed. When he got onto the truth, they murdered him.'

Angeli looked at Judd, a thoughtful frown on his face.

'That's why the killer is not going to stop until I'm dead,' Judd concluded quietly. 'It's become a deadly game, and the man I've described can't stand losing.'

Angeli was studying him, weighing what Judd had said. 'If you're right,' he said finally, 'you're going to need protection.' He took his service revolver out, flipped the chamber open to make sure it was fully loaded.

'Thanks, Angeli, but I don't need a gun. I'm going to fight them with my own weapons.'

There was a sharp click of the outer door opening. 'Were you expecting anyone?'

Judd shook his head. 'No. I have no patients this afternoon.'

Gun still in hand, Angeli moved quietly to the door leading to the reception room. He stepped to one side and yanked the door open. Peter Hadley stood there, a bewildered expression on his face. 'Who are you?' Angeli snapped.

Judd moved over to the door. 'It's all right,' Judd said quickly. 'He's a friend of mine.'

'Hey! What the hell goes?' asked Peter.

'Sorry,' Angeli apologized. He put his gun away.

'This is Dr Peter Hadley – Detective Angeli.'

'What kind of nutty psychiatric clinic are you running here?' Peter asked.

'There's been a little trouble,' Angeli explained. 'Dr Stevens' office has been . . . burgled, and we thought whoever did it might be returning.'

Judd picked up the cue. 'Yes. They didn't find what they were looking for.'

'Does this have anything to do with Carol's murder?' Peter asked.

Angeli spoke before Judd could answer. 'We're not sure, Dr Hadley. For the moment, the Department has asked Dr Stevens not to discuss the case.'

'I understand,' Peter said. He looked at Judd. 'Is our luncheon date still on?'

Judd realized he had forgotten about it. 'Of course,' he said quickly. He turned to Angeli. 'I think we've covered everything.'

'And then some,' Angeli agreed. 'You're sure you don't want . . .' He indicated his revolver.

Judd shook his head. 'Thanks.'

'Okay. Be careful,' Angeli said.

'I will,' Judd promised. 'I will.'

Judd was preoccupied during luncheon, and Peter did not press him. They talked of mutual friends, patients that they had in common. Peter told Judd he had

162

spoken to Harrison Burke's employer and it had been quietly arranged for Burke to have a mental examination. He was being sent to a private institution.

Over coffee Peter said, 'I don't know what kind of trouble you're having, Judd, but if I can be of any help . . .'

Judd shook his head. 'Thanks, Peter. This is something I have to take care of myself. I'll tell you all about it when it's over.'

'I hope that's soon,' Peter said lightly. He hesitated. 'Judd – are you in any danger?'

'Of course not,' replied Judd.

Unless you counted a homicidal maniac who had committed three murders and was determined to make Judd his fourth victim.

Chapter Fifteen

After lunch Judd returned to his office. He went through the same careful routine, checking to make sure that he exposed himself to minimum vulnerability.

For whatever that was worth.

He began going through the tapes again, listening for anything that might provide some clue. It was like turning on a torrent of verbal graffiti. The gusher of sounds that spewed forth was filled with hatred . . . perversion . . . fear . . . self-pity . . . megalomania . . . loneliness . . . emptiness . . . pain . . .

At the end of three hours he had found only one new name to add to his list: Bruce Boyd, the man with whom John Hanson had last lived. He put the Hanson tape on the recorder again.

'. . . I suppose I fell in love with Bruce the first time I saw him. He was the most beautiful man I had ever seen.'

'Was he the passive or dominant partner, John?'

'Dominant. That's one of the things that attracted me to him. He's very strong. In fact, later, when we became lovers, we used to quarrel about that.'

'Why?'

'Bruce didn't realize how strong he really was. He used to walk up behind me and hit me on the back. He meant it as a loving gesture, but one day he almost broke my spine. I wanted to kill him. When he shook hands, he would crush your fingers. He always pretended to be sorry, but Bruce enjoys hurting people. He didn't need whips. He's very strong . . .'

Judd stopped the tape and sat there, thinking. The homosexual pattern did not fit into his concept of the killer, but on the other hand, Boyd had been involved with Hanson and was a sadist and an egotist.

He looked at the two names on his list: Teri Washburn, who had killed a man in Hollywood and had never mentioned it; and Bruce Boyd, John Hanson's last lover. If it were one of them – which one?

Teri Washburn lived in a penthouse suite on Sutton Place. The entire apartment was decorated in shocking pink: walls, furniture, drapes. There were expensive pieces scattered around the room, and the wall was covered with French impressionists. Judd recognized two Manets, two Degas, a Monet, and a Renoir before Teri walked into the room. He had phoned her to tell her that he wanted to come by. She had got ready for him. She was wearing a wispy pink negligee with nothing on underneath it.

'You really came,' she exclaimed happily.

'I wanted to talk to you.'

'Sure. A little drinkie?'

'No, thanks.'

'Then I think I'll fix myself one to celebrate,' Teri said. She moved towards the coral-shell bar in the corner of the large living-room.

Judd watched her thoughtfully.

She returned with her drink and sat next to him on the pink couch. 'So your cock finally got you up here,

165

honey,' she said. 'I knew you couldn't hold out on little Teri. I'm nuts about you, Judd. I'd do anything for you. You name it. You make all the crummy pricks I've known in my life look like dirt.' She put her drink down and put her hand on his trousers.

Judd took her hands in his. 'Teri,' he said. 'I need your help.'

Her mind was travelling in its own groove. 'I know, baby,' she moaned. 'I'm going to fuck you like you've never been fucked in your life.'

'Teri – listen to me! Someone is trying to murder me!'

Her eyes registered slow surprise. Acting – or real? He remembered a performance he had seen her give on one of the late late shows. Real. She was good, but not that good an actress.

'For Christ sake! Who – Who'd want to murder *you*?'

'It could be someone connected with one of my patients.'

'But – Jesus – why?'

'That's what I'm trying to find out, Teri. Have any of your friends ever talked about killing . . . or murder? Maybe as a party game, for laughs?'

Teri shook her head. 'No.'

'Do you know anyone named Don Vinton?' He watched her closely.

'Don Vinton? Uhn-uhn. Should I?'

'Teri – how do you feel about murder?' A small shiver went through her body. He was holding her wrists and he could feel her pulse racing. 'Does murder excite you?'

'I don't know.'

'Think about it,' Judd insisted. 'Does the thought of it excite you?'

Her pulse was beginning to skip irregularly. 'No! Of course not.'

'Why didn't you tell me about the man you killed in Hollywood?'

Without warning she reached out to rake his face with her long fingernails. He grabbed her wrists.

'You rotten sonofabitch! That was twenty years ago . . . So that's why you came. Get out of here. Get out!' She collapsed in sobbing hysteria.

Judd watched her a moment. Teri was capable of being involved in a thrill murder. Her insecurity, her total lack of self-esteem, would make her easy prey to anyone who wanted to use her. She was like a piece of soft clay lying in the gutter. The person who picked her up could mould her into a beautiful statue – or into a deadly weapon. The question was, who had picked her up last? Don Vinton?

Judd got to his feet. 'I'm sorry,' he said.

He walked out of the pink apartment.

Bruce Boyd occupied a house in a converted mews off the park in Greenwich Village. The door was opened by a white-jacketed Filipino butler. Judd gave his name and was invited to wait in the foyer. The butler disappeared. Ten minutes went by, then fifteen. Judd checked his irritation. Perhaps he should have told Detective Angeli he was coming here. If Judd's theory was right, the next attempt on his life would take place very soon. And his attacker would try to make certain of his success.

The butler reappeared. 'Mr Boyd will see you now,'

he said. He led Judd upstairs to a tastefully decorated study, then discreetly withdrew.

Boyd was at a desk, writing. He was a beautiful man with sharp, delicate features, an aquiline nose, and a sensuous, full mouth. He had blond hair curled into ringlets. He got to his feet as Judd entered. He was about six foot three with the chest and shoulders of a football player. Judd thought about his physical identikit of the killer. Boyd matched it. Judd wished more than ever that he had left some word with Angeli.

Boyd's voice was soft and cultured. 'Forgive me for keeping you waiting, Dr Stevens,' he said pleasantly. 'I'm Bruce Boyd.' He held out his hand.

Judd reached out to take it and Boyd hit him in the mouth with a granite fist. The blow was totally unexpected, and the impact of it sent Judd crashing against a standing lamp, knocking it over as his body fell to the floor.

'I'm sorry, Doctor,' said Boyd, looking down at him. 'You had that coming. You've been a naughty boy, haven't you? Get up and I'll fix you a drink.'

Judd shook his head groggily. He started to push himself up from the floor. When he got halfway up, Boyd kicked him in the groin with the tip of his shoe and Judd fell writhing to the floor in agony. 'I've been waiting for you to call,' Boyd said.

Judd looked up through the blinding waves of pain at the figure that towered over him. He tried to speak, but he couldn't get the words out.

'Don't try to talk,' Boyd said sympathetically. 'It must hurt. I know why you're here. You want to ask me about Johnny.'

Judd started to nod and Boyd kicked him in the head. Through a red blur he heard Boyd's voice coming from some distant place through a cottony filter, fading in and out. 'We loved each other until he went to you. You made him feel like a freak. You made him feel our love was dirty. Do you know who made it dirty, Dr Stevens? You.'

Judd felt something hard smash into his ribs, sending an exquisite river of pain through his veins. He was seeing everything in beautiful colours now, as though his head were filled with shimmering rainbows.

'Who gave you the right to tell people how to love, Doctor? You sit there in your office like some kind of god, condemning everyone who doesn't think like you.'

That's not true, Judd was answering somewhere in his mind. *Hanson had never had choices before. I gave him choices. And he didn't choose you.*

'Now Johnny's dead,' said the blond giant towering over him. 'You killed my Johnny. And now I'm going to kill you.'

He felt another kick behind his ear, and he began to slip into unconsciousness. Some remote part of his mind watched with a detached interest as the rest of him began to die. That small isolated piece of intelligence in his cerebellum continued to function, its impulses flashing out weakening patterns of thought. He reproached himself for not having come closer to the truth. He had expected the killer to be a dark, Latin type, and he was blond. He had been sure that the killer was not a homosexual, and he had been wrong.

169

He had found his homicidal maniac, and now he was
going to die for it.

He lost consciousness.

Chapter Sixteen

Some distant, remote part of his mind was trying to send him a message, trying to communicate something of cosmic importance, but the hammering deep inside his skull was so agonizing that he was unable to concentrate on anything else. Somewhere nearby, he could hear a high-pitched keening, like a wounded wild animal. Slowly, painfully, Judd opened his eyes. He was lying in a bed in a strange room. In a corner of the room, Bruce Boyd was weeping uncontrollably.

Judd started to sit up. The wracking pain in his body flooded his memory with recollection of what had happened to him, and he was suddenly filled with a wild, savage fury.

Boyd turned as he heard Judd stir. He walked over to the bed. 'It's your fault,' he whimpered. 'If it hadn't been for you, Johnny would still be safe with me.'

Without volition, propelled by some long-forgotten, deeply buried instinct for vengeance, Judd reached for Boyd's throat, his fingers closing around his windpipe, squeezing with all their strength. Boyd made no move to protect himself. He stood there, tears streaming down his face. Judd looked into his eyes, and it was like looking into a pool of hell. Slowly his hands dropped away. *My God*, he thought, *I'm a doctor. A sick man attacks me and I want to kill him*. He looked at Boyd, and he was looking at a destroyed, bewildered child.

And suddenly he realized what his subconscious had been trying to tell him: Bruce Boyd was not Don Vinton. If he had been, Judd would not be alive now. Boyd was incapable of committing murder. So he had been right about him not fitting the identikit of the killer. There was a certain ironic consolation in that.

'If it weren't for you, Johnny would be alive,' Boyd sobbed. 'He'd be here with me and I could have protected him.'

'I didn't ask John Hanson to leave you,' Judd said wearily. 'It was his idea.'

'You're a liar!'

'Things had been going wrong between you and John *before* he came to see me.'

There was a long silence. Then Boyd nodded. 'Yes. We – we were quarrelling all the time.'

'He was trying to find himself, and his instincts kept telling him that he wanted to go back to his wife and children. Deep down inside, John wanted to be heterosexual.'

'Yes,' whispered Boyd. 'He used to talk about it all the time, and I thought it was just to punish me.' He looked up at Judd. 'But one day he left me. He just – moved out. He stopped loving me.' There was despair in his voice.

'He didn't stop loving you,' Judd said. 'Not as a friend.'

Boyd was looking at him now, his eyes riveted on Judd's face. 'Will you help me?' His eyes were filled with desperation. 'H-help me. You've got to help me!'

It was a cry of anguish. Judd looked at him a long moment. 'Yes.' Judd said. 'I'll help you.'

'Will I be normal?'

'There's no such thing as normal. Each person carries his own normality within him, and no two people are alike.'

'Can you make me heterosexual?'

'That depends on how much you really want to be. We can give you psychoanalysis.'

'And if it fails?'

'If we find that you're meant to be homosexual, at least you'll be better adjusted to it.'

'When can we start?' Boyd asked.

And Judd was jolted back to reality. He was sitting here talking about treating a patient when, for all he knew, he was going to be murdered within the next twenty-four hours. And he was still no closer to finding out who Don Vinton was. He had eliminated Teri and Boyd, the last suspects on his list. He knew no more now than when he had started. If his analysis of the killer was correct, by now he would have worked himself up to a murderous rage. The next attack would come very, very soon.

'Call me Monday,' he said.

As the taxi took him towards his apartment building, Judd tried to weigh his chances of survival. They looked bleak. What could he have that Don Vinton wanted so desperately? And who was Don Vinton? How could he have had no police record? Could he be using some other name? No. Moody had clearly said 'Don Vinton'.

It was difficult to concentrate. Every movement of the taxi sent spasms of excruciating pain through his bruised body. Judd thought about the murders and attempted murders that had been committed so far, looking for some kind of pattern that made sense. A knifing, murder by torture, a hit-and-run 'accident', a bomb in his car, strangulation. There was no pattern that he could discern. Only a ruthless, maniacal violence. He had no way of knowing how the next attempt would be made. Or by whom. His greatest vulnerability would be the office and his apartment. He remembered Angeli's advice. He must have stronger locks put on the doors of the apartment. He would tell Mike, the doorman, and Eddie, the elevator operator, to keep their eyes open. He could trust them.

The taxi pulled up in front of his apartment house. The doorman opened the taxi door.

He was a total stranger.

Chapter Seventeen

He was a large, swarthy man with a pockmarked face and deep-set black eyes. An old scar ran across his throat. He was wearing Mike's uniform coat and it was too tight for him.

The taxi pulled away and Judd was alone with the man. He was struck by a sudden wave of pain. My God, not now! He gritted his teeth. 'Where's Mike?' he asked.

'On vacation, Doctor.'

Doctor. So the man knew who he was. And Mike on vacation? In December?

There was a small smile of satisfaction on the man's face. Judd looked up and down the windswept street, but it was completely deserted. He could try to make a run for it, but in his condition he wouldn't stand a chance. His body was beaten and sore, and it hurt every time he took a breath.

'You look like you been in an accident.' The man's voice was almost genial.

Judd turned without answering and walked into the lobby of the apartment building. He could count on Eddie to get help.

The doorman followed Judd into the lobby. Eddie was in the elevator, his back turned. Judd started walking towards the elevator, every step a separate agony. He knew he dared not falter now. The important thing was not to let the man catch him alone. He would be afraid of witnesses. 'Eddie!' Judd called.

The man in the elevator turned.

Judd had never seen him before. He was a smaller version of the doorman, except that there was no scar. It was obvious that the two men were brothers.

Judd stopped, trapped between the two of them. There was no one else in the lobby.

'Goin' up,' said the man in the elevator. He had the same satisfied smile as his brother.

So these, finally, were the faces of death. Judd was sure that neither of them was the brain behind what was happening. They were hired professional killers. Would they kill him in the lobby, or would they prefer to do it in his apartment? His apartment, he reasoned. That would give them more time to make their escape before his body was found.

Judd took a step towards the manager's office. 'I have to see Mr Katz about – '

The larger man blocked his way. 'Mr Katz is busy, Doc,' he said softly.

The man in the elevator spoke. 'I'll take you upstairs.'

'No,' Judd said. 'I – '

'Do like he says.' There was no emotion in his voice.

There was a sudden blast of cold air as the lobby door opened. Two men and two women hurried in, laughing and chattering, huddled in their coats.

'It's worse than Siberia,' said one of the women.

The man holding her arm was pudgy-faced, with a Mid-western accent. 'Tain't a fit night for man nor beast.'

The group was moving towards the elevator. The

doorman and elevator operator looked at each other silently.

The second woman spoke. She was a tiny, platinum blonde with a heavy Southern accent. 'It's been a perfectly dreamy evening. Thank you all so much.' She was sending the men away.

The second man gave a howl of protest. 'You're not going to let us go without a little night cap, are you?'

'It's awfully late, George,' simpered the first woman.

'But it's below zero outside. You've gotta give us a little anti-freeze.'

The other man added his plea. 'Just one drink and then we go.'

'Well . . .'

Judd was holding his breath. *Please!*

The platinum blonde relented. 'All right. But just one, you-all hear?'

Laughing, the group stepped into the elevator. Judd quickly moved in with them. The doorman stood there uncertainly, looking at his brother. The one in the elevator shrugged, closed the door, and started the elevator up. Judd's apartment was on the fifth floor. If the group got out before him, he was in trouble. If they got out after him, he had a chance to get into his apartment, barricade himself, and call for help.

'Floor?'

The little blonde giggled. 'I don't know what my husband would say if he saw me inviting two strange men up to my apartment.' She turned to the elevator operator. 'Ten.'

Judd exhaled and realized that he had been holding his breath. He spoke quickly. 'Five.'

The elevator operator gave him a patient, knowing look and opened the door at Five. Judd got out. The elevator door closed.

Judd moved towards his apartment, stumbling with pain. He took out his key, opened the door, and went in, his heart pounding. He had five minutes at the most before they came to kill him. He closed the door and started to put the chain lock in the bolt. It came off in his hand. He looked at it and saw that it had been cut through. He flung it down and moved towards the phone. A wave of dizziness swept over him. He stood there, fighting the pain, his eyes closed, while precious time passed. With an effort, he started towards the phone again, moving slowly. The only person he could think of to call was Angeli, but Angeli was at home, ill. Besides – what could he say? *We have a new doorman and elevator operator and I think they're going to kill me?* He slowly became aware that he was holding the receiver in his hand, standing there numbly, too dazed to do anything. Concussion, he thought. Boyd may have killed me, after all. They would walk in and find him like this – helpless. He remembered the look in the eyes of the big man. He had to out-wit them, keep them off balance. But good God – how?

He turned on the small TV set that monitored the lobby. The lobby was deserted. The pain returned, washing over him in waves, making him feel faint. He forced his tired mind to focus on the problem. He was in an emergency . . . Yes . . . Emergency. He had to take emergency measures. Yes . . . His vision was blurring again. His eyes focused on the phone. Emergency . . . He moved the dial close to his eyes so that he could read the numbers. Slowly, painfully, he dialled.

A voice answered on the fifth ring. Judd spoke, his words slurred and indistinct. His eye was caught by a flurry of motion in the TV monitor. The two men, in street clothes, were crossing the lobby and moving towards the elevator.

His time had run out.

The two men moved soundlessly towards Judd's apartment and took positions on either side of the door. The larger of the men, Rocky, softly tried the door. It was locked. He took out a celluloid card and carefully inserted it over the lock. He nodded to his brother, and both men took out revolvers with silencers on them. Rocky slid the celluloid card inside the lock and pushed the unresisting door open, slowly. They walked into the living-room, guns held out in front of them. They were confronted by three closed doors. There was no sign of Judd. The smaller brother, Nick, tried the first door. It was locked. He smiled at his brother, put the muzzle of his gun against the lock, and pulled the trigger. The door noiselessly swung open into a bedroom. The two men moved inside, guns sweeping the room.

There was no one inside. Nick checked the closets while Rocky returned to the living-room. They moved without haste, knowing that Judd was in the apartment hiding, helpless. There was almost deliberate enjoyment in their unhurried movements, as though they were savouring the moments before the kill.

Nick tried the second closed door. It was locked. He shot the bolt out and moved into the room. It was the den. Empty. They grinned at each other and walked towards the last closed door. As they passed the TV monitor, Rocky caught his brother's arm. On the set they could see three men hurrying into the lobby. Two of them, wearing the white jackets of interns, were pushing a wheeled stretcher. The third carried a medical bag.

'What the hell!'

'Keep your cool, Rocky. So someone's sick. There must be a hundred apartments in this building.'

They watched the TV set in fascination as the two interns wheeled the stretcher into the elevator. The group disappeared inside it, and the elevator door closed.

'Give them a couple of minutes.' It was Nick. 'It could be some kind of accident. That means there might be cops.'

'Of all the fuckin' luck!'

'Don't worry. Stevens ain't goin' nowhere.'

The door to the apartment burst open and the doctor and the two interns entered, pushing the stretcher ahead of them. Swiftly the two killers shoved their guns into their overcoat pockets.

The doctor walked up to the brothers, 'Is he dead?'

'Who?'

'The suicide victim. Is he dead or alive?'

The two killers looked at each other, bewildered. 'You guys got the wrong apartment.'

The doctor pushed past the two killers and tried the bedroom door. 'It's locked. Help me break it down.'

The two brothers watched helplessly as the doctor and the interns smashed the door open with their shoulders. The doctor stepped into the bedroom. 'Bring the stretcher.' He moved to the bedside where Judd lay on the bed. 'Are you all right?'

Judd looked up, trying to make his eyes focus. 'Hospital,' mumbled Judd.

'You're on your way.'

As the two killers watched in frustration, the interns wheeled the stretcher into the bedroom, skilfully slid Judd onto it, and wrapped him in blankets.

'Let's blow,' said Rocky.

The doctor watched the two men leave. Then he turned to Judd, who lay on the stretcher, his face white and haggard. 'Are you all right, Judd?' His voice was filled with deep concern.

Judd tried a smile that didn't come off. 'Great,' he said. He could scarcely hear his own voice. 'Thanks, Pete.'

Peter looked down at his friend, then nodded to the two interns. 'Let's go!'

Chapter Eighteen

The hospital room was different, but the nurse was the same. A glaring bundle of disapproval. Seated at his bedside, she was the first thing that Judd saw when he opened his eyes.

'Well. We're up,' she said primly. 'Dr Harris wants to see you. I'll tell him we're awake.' She walked stiffly out of the room.

Judd sat up, moving carefully. Arm and leg reflexes a bit slow, but unimpaired. He tried focusing on a chair across the room, one eye at a time. His vision was a little blurred.

'Want a consultation?'

He looked up. Dr Seymour Harris had come into the room.

'Well,' Dr Harris said cheerfully, 'you're turning out to be one of our best customers. Do you know how much your stitching bill alone is? We're going to have to give you discount rates . . . How did you sleep, Judd?' He sat down on the edge of the bed.

'Like a baby. What did you give me?'

'A shot of sodium luminol.'

'What time is it?'

'Noon.'

'My God,' Judd said. 'I've got to get out of here.'

Dr Harris removed the chart from the clipboard he

carried. 'What would you like to talk about first? Your concussion? Lacerations? Contusions?'

'I feel fine.'

The doctor put the chart aside. His voice grew serious. 'Judd, your body's taken a lot of punishment. More than you realize. If you're smart, you'll stay right in this bed for a few days and rest. Then you'll take a vacation for a month.'

'Thanks, Seymour,' Judd said.

'You mean thanks, but – no, thanks.'

'There's something I have to take care of.'

Dr Harris sighed. 'Do you know who make the worst patients in the world? Doctors.' He changed the subject, conceding defeat. 'Peter was here all night. He's been calling every hour. He's worried about you. He thinks someone tried to kill you last night.'

'You know how doctors are – over-imaginative.'

Harris eyed him a moment, shrugged, then said, 'You're the analyst. I'm only Ben Casey. Maybe you know what you're doing – but I wouldn't bet a nickel on it. Are you sure you won't stay in bed a few days?'

'I can't.'

'Okay, Tiger. I'll let you leave tomorrow.'

Judd started to protest, but Harris cut him off.

'Don't argue. Today's Sunday. The guys who beat you up need a rest.'

'Seymour . . .'

'Another thing. I hate to sound like a Jewish mother, but have you been eating lately?'

'Not much,' Judd said.

'Okay. I'm giving Miss Bedpan twenty-four hours to fatten you up. And Judd . . .'

'Yes?'

'Be careful. I hate to lose such a good customer.' And Dr Harris was gone.

Judd closed his eyes to rest a moment. He heard the rattle of dishes, and when he looked up, a beautiful Irish nurse was wheeling in a dining tray.

'You're awake, Dr Stevens.' She smiled.

'What time is it?'

'Six o'clock.'

He had slept the day away.

She was placing the food on his bed tray. 'You're having a treat tonight – turkey. Tomorrow's Christmas Eve.'

'I know.' He had no appetite for dinner until he took the first bite and suddenly discovered that he was ravenous. Dr Harris had shut off all phone calls, so he lay in bed, undisturbed, gathering his strength, marshalling the forces within him. Tomorrow he would need all the energy he could muster.

At ten o'clock the next morning Dr Seymour Harris bustled into Judd's room. 'How's my favourite patient?' he beamed. 'You look almost human.'

'I feel almost human,' smiled Judd.

'Good. You're going to have a visitor. I wouldn't want you to scare him.'

Peter. And probably Norah. They seemed to be spending most of their time lately visiting him in hospitals.

Dr Harris went on. 'It's a Lieutenant McGreavy.'

Judd's heart sank.

'He's very anxious to talk to you. He's on his way over here. He wanted to be sure you were awake.'

So he could arrest him. With Angeli home sick, McGreavy had been free to manufacture evidence that would convict Judd. Once McGreavy got his hands on him, there was no hope. He had to escape before McGreavy arrived.

'Would you ask the nurse to get the barber?' Judd said. 'I'd like a shave.' His voice must have sounded odd, because Dr Harris was looking at him strangely. Or was that because of something McGreavy had told Dr Harris about him?

'Certainly, Judd.' He left.

The moment the door closed, Judd got out of bed and stood up. The two nights of sleep had done miracles for him. He was a little unsteady on his feet, but that would pass. Now he had to move quickly. It took him three minutes to dress.

He opened the door a crack, made sure that no one was around who would try to stop him, and headed for the service stairs. As he started down the stairs, the elevator door opened and he saw McGreavy get off and start towards the room he had just left. He was moving swiftly, and behind him were a uniformed policeman and two detectives. Quickly, Judd went down the stairs and headed for the ambulance entrance. A block away from the hospital he hailed a taxi.

McGreavy walked into the hospital room and took one look at the unoccupied bed and the empty closet. 'Fan out,' he said to the others. 'You might still catch him.' He scooped up the phone. The operator connected him with the police switchboard. 'This is McGreavy,' he said rapidly. 'I want an all-points bulletin put out. Urgent . . . Dr Stevens, Judd. Male. Caucasian. Age . . .'

The taxi pulled up in front of Judd's office building. From now on, there was no safety for him anywhere. He could not go back to his apartment. He would have to check into some hotel. Returning to his office was dangerous, but it had to be done this once.

He needed a phone number.

He paid the driver and walked into the lobby. Every muscle in his body ached. He moved quickly. He knew he had very little time. It was unlikely that they would be expecting him to return to his office, but he must take no chances. It was now a question of who got him first. The police or his assassins.

When he reached his office, he opened the door and went inside, locking the door after him. The inner office seemed strange and hostile, and Judd knew that he could not treat his patients here any longer. He would be subjecting them to too much danger. He was filled with anger at what Don Vinton was doing to his life. He could visualize the scene that must have occurred when the two brothers went back and reported that they had failed to kill him. If he had read Don Vinton's character correctly, he would have been in a towering rage. The next attack would come at any moment.

Judd went across the room to get Anne's phone number. For he had remembered two things in the hospital.

Some of Anne's appointments were scheduled just ahead of John Hanson's.

And Anne and Carol had had several chats together; Carol might have innocently confided some deadly information to Anne. If so, she could be in danger.

He took his address book out of a locked drawer, looked up Anne's phone number, and dialled. There were three rings, and then a neutral voice came on.

'This is a special operator. What number are you calling, please?'

Judd gave her the number. A few moments later the operator was back on the line. 'I am sorry. You are calling a wrong number. Please check your directory or consult Information.'

'Thank you,' Judd said. He hung up. He sat there a moment, remembering what his answering service had said a few days ago. *They had been able to reach all his patients except Anne.* The numbers could have been transposed when they were put in the book. He looked in the telephone directory, but there was no listing under her husband's name or her name. He suddenly felt that it was very important that he talk to Anne. He copied down her address: 617 Woodside Avenue, Bayonne, New Jersey.

Fifteen minutes later, he was at an Avis counter, renting a car. There was a sign behind the counter that read: 'We're second, so we try harder.' *We're in the same boat,* thought Judd.

A few minutes later, he drove out of the garage. He rode around the block, satisfied himself that he was not being followed, and headed over the George Washington Bridge for New Jersey.

When he reached Bayonne, he stopped at a filling station to ask directions. 'Next corner and make a left – third street.'

'Thanks.' Judd drove off. At the thought of seeing Anne again, his heart began to quicken. What was he going to say to her without alarming her? Would her husband be there?

Judd made a left turn onto Woodside Avenue. He looked at the numbers. He was in the nine hundred block. The houses on both sides of the street were small, old, and weatherbeaten. He drove to the seven hundred block. The houses seemed to become progressively older and smaller.

Anne lived on a beautiful wooded estate. There were virtually no trees here. When Judd reached the address Anne had given him, he was almost prepared for what he saw.

617 was a weed-covered vacant lot.

Chapter Nineteen

He sat in the car across from the vacant lot, trying to put it all together. The wrong phone number could have been a mistake. Or the address could have been a mistake. But not both. Anne had deliberately lied to him. And if she had lied about who she was and where she lived, what else had she lied about? He forced himself to objectively examine everything he really knew about her. It came to almost nothing. She had walked into his office unannounced and insisted on becoming a patient. In the four weeks that she had been coming to him, she had carefully managed not to reveal what her problem was, and then had suddenly announced that it was solved and she was going away. After each visit she had paid him in cash so that there would be no way of tracing her. But what reason could she have had for posing as a patient and then vanishing? There was only one answer. And as it hit Judd, he became physically sick.

If someone wanted to set him up for murder – wanted to know his routine at the office – wanted to know what the inside of the office looked like – what better way than to gain access as a patient? That was what she was doing there. Don Vinton had sent her. She had learned what she needed to know and then had disappeared without a trace.

It had all been pretence, and how eager he had been

189

to be taken in by it. How she must have laughed when she went back to report to Don Vinton about the amorous idiot who called himself an analyst and pretended to be an expert about people. He was head over heels in love with a girl whose sole interest in him was setting him up to be murdered. How was *that* for a judge of character? What an amusing paper that would make for the American Psychiatric Association.

But what if it were not true? Supposing Anne had come to him with a legitimate problem, had used a fictitious name because she was afraid of embarrassing someone? In time the problem had solved itself and she had decided that she no longer needed the help of an analyst. But Judd knew that it was too easy. There was an 'x' quantity about Anne that needed to be discovered. He had a strong feeling that in that unknown quantity could lie the answer to what was happening. It was possible that she was being forced to act against her will. But even as he thought it, he knew he was being foolish. He was trying to cast her as a damsel in distress with himself as a knight in shining armour. Had she set him up for murder? Somehow, he had to find out.

An elderly woman in a torn housecoat had come out of a house across the street and was staring at him. He turned the car around and headed back for the George Washington Bridge.

There was a line of cars behind him. Any one of them could be following him. But why would they have to follow him? His enemies knew where to find him. He couldn't sit and passively wait for them to attack. He had to do the attacking himself, keep them off guard, enrage Don Vinton into making a blunder so that he could be checkmated. And he had to do it before McGreavy caught him and locked him up.

Judd drove towards Manhattan. The only possible key to all this was Anne – and she had disappeared without a trace. The day after tomorrow she would be out of the country.

And Judd suddenly realized that he had one chance of finding her.

It was Christmas Eve and the Pan-Am office was crowded with travellers and would-be travellers on standby, fighting to get space on planes flying all over the world.

Judd made his way to the counter through the waiting lines and asked to see the manager. The uniformed girl behind the counter gave him a professionally coded smile and asked him to wait; the manager was on the phone.

Judd stood there hearing a babel of phrases.

'I want to leave India on the fifth.'

'Will Paris be cold?'

'I want a car to meet me in Lisbon.'

He felt a desperate desire to get on a plane and run away. He suddenly realized how exhausted he was, physically and emotionally. Don Vinton seemed to have an army at his disposal, but Judd was alone. What chance did he have against him?

'Can I help you?'

Judd turned. A tall, cadaverous-looking man stood behind the counter. 'I'm Friendly,' he said. He waited for Judd to appreciate the joke. Judd smiled dutifully. 'Charles Friendly. What can I do for you?'

'I'm Dr Stevens. I'm trying to locate a patient of mine. She's booked on a flight leaving for Europe tomorrow.'

'The name?'

'Blake. Anne Blake.' He hesitated. 'Possibly it's under Mr and Mrs Anthony Blake.'

'What city is she flying to?'

'I – I'm not sure.'

'Are they booked on one of our morning or afternoon flights?'

'I'm not even certain if it's with your airline,' Judd said.

The friendliness dropped out of Mr Friendly's eyes. 'Then I'm afraid I can't help you.'

Judd felt a sudden feeling of panic. 'It's really urgent. I must find her before she goes.'

'Doctor, Pan-American has one or more flights leaving every day for Amsterdam, Barcelona, Berlin, Brussels, Copenhagen, Dublin, Düsseldorf, Frankfurt, Hamburg, Lisbon, London, Munich, Paris, Rome, Shannon, Stuttgart, and Vienna. So have most of the other international airlines. You'll have to contact each one individually. And I doubt if they can help you unless you can give them the destination and time of departure.' The expression on Mr Friendly's face was one of impatience. 'If you'll excuse me . . .' He turned to walk away.

'Wait!' said Judd. How could he explain that this might be his last chance to stay alive? His last link to finding out who was attempting to kill him.

Friendly was regarding him with barely concealed annoyance. 'Yes?'

Judd forced a smile on his face, hating himself for it.

'Don't you have some kind of central computing system,' he asked, 'where you can get passengers' names by . . . ?'

'Only if you know the flight number,' Mr Friendly said. He turned and was gone.

Judd stood there at the counter, feeling sick. Check and checkmate. He was defeated. There was nowhere else to move.

A group of Italian priests bustled in, dressed in long, flapping black robes and wide black hats, looking like something out of the Middle Ages. They were weighed down with cheap cardboard suitcases, boxes and gift baskets of fruit. They were speaking loudly in Italian and obviously teasing the youngest member of their group, a boy who looked no more than eighteen or nineteen. They were probably returning home to Rome after a vacation, thought Judd, as he listened to their babbling. Rome . . . where Anne would be . . . Anne again.

The priests were moving towards the counter.

'*E molto bene di ritornare a casa.*'

'*Si, d'accordo.*'

'*Signore, per piacere, guardatemi.*'

'*Tutto va bene?*'

'*Si, ma –*'

'*Dio mio, dove sono i miei biglietti?*'

'*Cretino, hai perduto i biglietti.*'

'*Ah, eccoli.*'

The priests handed their airline tickets to the youngest priest, who moved bashfully towards the girl at the counter. Judd looked towards the exit. A large man in a grey overcoat was lounging in the doorway.

The young priest was talking to the girl behind the counter. *'Dieci. Dieci.'*

The girl stared at him blankly. The priest summoned up his knowledge of English and said very carefully, 'Ten. Billetta. Teeket.' He pushed the tickets towards her.

The girl smiled happily and began to process the tickets. The priests burst into delighted cries of approval at their companion's linguistic abilities and clapped him on the back.

There was no point in staying here any longer. Sooner or later he would have to face whatever was out there. Judd slowly turned and started to move past the group of priests.

'Guardate che ha fatto il Don Vinton.'

Judd stopped, the blood suddenly rushing to his face. He turned to the tubby little priest who had spoken and took his arm. 'Excuse me,' he said. His voice was hoarse and unsteady. 'Did you say "Don Vinton"?'

The priest looked up at him blankly, then patted him on the arm and started to move away.

Judd tightened his grip. 'Wait!' he said.

The priest was looking at him nervously. Judd forced himself to speak calmly. 'Don Vinton. Which one is he? Show him to me.'

All the priests were now staring at Judd. The little priest looked at his companions. *'E un americano matto.'*

A babble of excited Italian rose from the group. Out of the corner of his eye, Judd saw Friendly watching him from behind the counter. Friendly opened the counter gate and started to move towards him. Judd fought to control a rising panic. He let go of the priest's arm, leaned close to him, and said slowly and distinctly, 'Don Vinton.'

The little priest looked into Judd's face for a moment and then his own face splintered into merriment. '*Don Vinton!*'

The manager was approaching rapidly, his manner hostile. Judd nodded to the priest encouragingly. The little priest pointed to the boy. '*Don Vinton* – "big man".'

And suddenly the puzzle fell into place.

Chapter Twenty

'Slow down, slow down,' Angeli said hoarsely. 'I can't understand a word you're saying.'

'Sorry,' Judd said. He took a deep breath. 'I've got the answer!' He was so relieved to hear Angeli's voice over the phone that he was almost babbling. 'I know who's trying to kill me. I know who Don Vinton is.'

There was a sceptical note in Angeli's voice. 'We couldn't find any Don Vinton.'

'Do you know why? Because it isn't a him – it's a *who*.'

'Will you speak more slowly?'

Judd's voice was trembling with excitement. 'Don Vinton isn't a name. It's an Italian expression. It means "the big man". That's what Moody was trying to tell me. That The Big Man was after me.'

'You lost me, Doctor.'

'It doesn't mean anything in English,' said Judd, 'but when you say it in Italian – doesn't it suggest anything to you? An organization of killers run by The Big Man?'

There was a long silence over the phone. 'La Cosa Nostra?'

'Who else could assemble a group of killers and weapons like that? Acid, bombs – guns! Remember I told you the man we're looking for would be a Southern European? He's Italian.'

'It doesn't make sense. Why would La Cosa Nostra want to kill you?'

'I have absolutely no idea. But I'm right. I know I'm right. And it fits in with something Moody said. He said there was a group of men out to kill me.'

'It's the craziest theory I've ever heard,' Angeli said. There was a pause, then he added, 'But I suppose it could be possible.'

Judd was flooded with sudden relief. If Angeli had not been willing to listen to him, he would have had no one to turn to.

'Have you discussed this with anyone?'

'No,' Judd said.

'Don't!' Angeli's voice was urgent. 'If you're right, your life depends on it. Don't go near your office or apartment.'

'I won't,' Judd promised. He suddenly remembered. 'Did you know McGreavy has a warrant out for my arrest?'

'Yes.' Angeli hesitated. 'If McGreavy picks you up, you'll never get to the station alive.'

My God! So he had been right about McGreavy. But he could not believe that McGreavy was the brain behind this. There was someone directing him . . . Don Vinton, The Big Man.

'Can you hear me?'

Judd's mouth was suddenly dry. 'Yes.'

A man in a grey overcoat stood outside the phone booth looking in at Judd. Was it the same man he had seen before? 'Angeli . . .'

'Yes?'

'I don't know who the others are. I don't know what they look like. How do I stay alive until they're caught?'

The man outside the booth was staring at him.

Angeli's voice came over the line. 'We're going straight to the FBI. I have a friend who has connections. He'll see that you're protected until you're safe. Okay?' There was a note of assurance in Angeli's voice.

'Okay,' Judd said gratefully. His knees felt like jelly.

'Where are you?'

'In a phone booth in the lower lobby of the Pan-Am Building.'

'Don't move. Keep plenty of people around you. I'm on my way.' There was a click at the other end of the line as Angeli hung up.

He put the phone back on the squad-room desk, a sick feeling deep inside him. Over the years he had become accustomed to dealing with murderers, rapists, perverts of every description, and somehow, in time, a protective shell had formed, allowing him to go on believing in the basic dignity and humanity of man.

But a rogue cop was something different.

A rogue cop was a corruption that touched everyone on the force, that violated everything that decent cops fought and died for.

The squad room was filled with the passage of feet and the murmur of voices, but he heard none of it. Two uniformed patrolmen passed through the room with a giant drunk in handcuffs. One of the officers had a black eye and the other had a handkerchief to a bloody nose. The sleeve of his uniform had been ripped half off. The patrolman would have to pay for that himself. These men were ready to risk their lives every day and night of the year. But that wasn't what made headlines. A crooked cop made headlines. One crooked cop tainted them all. His own partner.

Wearily he got up and walked down the ancient corridor to the Captain's office. He knocked once and went in.

Behind a battered desk pocked with the lighted cigar butts of countless years sat Captain Bertelli. Two FBI men were in the room, dressed in business suits. Captain Bertelli looked up as the door opened. 'Well?'

The detective nodded. 'It checks out. The property custodian said he came in and borrowed Carol Roberts's key from the evidence locker Wednesday afternoon and returned it late Wednesday night. That's why the paraffin test was negative – he got into Dr Stevens's office by using an original key. The custodian never questioned it because he knew he was assigned to the case.'

'Do you know where he is now?' asked the younger of the FBI men.

'No. We had a tail on him, but he lost him. He could be anywhere.'

'He'll be hunting for Dr Stevens,' said the second FBI agent.

Captain Bertelli turned to the FBI men. 'What are the chances of Dr Stevens staying alive?'

The man shook his head. 'If they find him before we do – none.'

Captain Bertelli nodded. 'We've got to find him first.' His voice grew savage. 'I want Angeli brought back, too. I don't care how you get him.' He turned to the detective. 'Just get him, McGreavy.'

*

The police radio began to crackle out a staccato message: 'Code Ten . . . Code Ten . . . All cars . . . pick up five . . .'

Angeli switched the radio off. 'Anyone know I picked you up?' he asked.

'No one,' Judd assured him.

'You haven't discussed La Cosa Nostra with anybody?'

'Only you.'

Angeli nodded, satisfied.

They had crossed the George Washington Bridge and were headed for New Jersey. But everything had changed. Before, he had been filled with apprehension. Now, with Angeli at his side, he no longer felt like the hunted. He was the hunter. And the thought filled him with deep satisfaction.

At Angeli's suggestion, Judd had left his rented car in Manhattan and he was riding in Angeli's unmarked police car. Angeli had headed north on the Palisades Interstate Parkway and exited at Orangeburg. They were approaching Old Tappan.

'It was smart of you to spot what was going on, Doctor,' Angeli said.

Judd shook his head. 'I should have figured it out as soon as I knew there was more than one man involved. It had to be an organization using professional killers. I think Moody suspected the truth when he saw the bomb in my car. They had access to every kind of weapon.'

And Anne. She was part of the operation, setting him up so that they could murder him. And yet – he couldn't hate her. No matter what she had done, he could never hate her.

Angeli had turned off the main highway. He deftly tooled the car onto a secondary road that led towards a wooded area.

'Does your friend know we're coming?' Judd asked.

'I phoned him. He's all ready for you.'

A side road appeared abruptly, and Angeli turned the car into it. He drove for a mile, then braked to a stop in front of an electric gate. Judd noticed a small television camera mounted above the gate. There was a click and the gate swung open, then closed solidly behind them. They began driving up a long, curving driveway. Through the trees ahead, Judd caught a glimpse of the sprawling roof of an enormous house. High on top, flashing in the sun, was a bronze rooster.

Its tail was missing.

Chapter Twenty-one

In the soundproofed, neon-lit communications centre at Police Headquarters, a dozen shirtsleeved police officers manned the giant switchboard. Six operators sat on each side of the board. In the middle of the board was a pneumatic chute. As the calls came in, the operators wrote a message, put it in the chute, and sent it upstairs to the dispatcher, for immediate relay to a sub-station or patrol car. The calls never ceased. They poured in day and night, like a river of tragedy flooding in from the citizens of the huge metropolis. Men and women who were terrified . . . lonely . . . desperate . . . drunk . . . injured . . . homicidal . . . It was a scene from Hogarth, painted with vivid, anguished words instead of colours.

On this Monday afternoon there was a feeling of added tension in the air. Each telephone operator handled his job with full concentration, and yet each was aware of the number of detectives and FBI agents who kept moving in and out of the room, receiving and giving orders, working efficiently and quietly as they spread a vast electronic net for Dr Judd Stevens and Detective Frank Angeli. The atmosphere was quickened, strangely staccato, as though the action were being staged by some grim, nervous puppeteer.

Captain Bertelli was talking to Allen Sullivan, a member of the Mayor's Crime Commission, when

McGreavy walked in. McGreavy had met Sullivan before. He was tough and honest. Bertelli broke off his conversation and turned to the detective, his face a question mark.

'Things are moving,' McGreavy said. 'We found an eye-witness, a night watchman who works in the building across the street from Dr Stevens's office building. On Wednesday night, when someone broke into Dr Stevens's office, the watchman was just going on duty. He saw two men go into the building. The street door was locked and they opened it with a key. He figured they worked there.'

'Did you get an ID?'

'He identified a picture of Angeli.'

'Wednesday night Angeli was supposed to have been home in bed with the flu.'

'Right.'

'What about the second man?'

'The watchman didn't get a good look at him.'

An operator plugged in one of the innumerable red lights blinking across the switchboard and turned to Captain Bertelli. 'For you, Captain. New Jersey Highway Patrol.'

Bertelli snatched up an extension phone. 'Captain Bertelli.' He listened a moment. 'Are you sure? . . . Good! Will you get every unit you can in there? Set up roadblocks. I want that area covered like a blanket. Keep in close touch . . . Thanks.' He hung up and turned to the two men. 'It looks like we got a break. A rookie patrolman in New Jersey spotted Angeli's car on a secondary road near Orangeburg. The Highway Patrol's combing the area now.'

'Dr Stevens?'

'He was in the car with Angeli. Don't worry. They'll find them.'

McGreavy pulled out two cigars. He offered one to Sullivan, who refused it, handed one to Bertelli, and put the other one between his teeth. 'We've got one thing going for us. Dr Stevens leads a charmed life.' He struck a match and lit the two cigars. 'I just talked to a friend of his – Dr Peter Hadley. Dr Hadley told me he went to pick up Stevens in his office a few days ago and found Angeli there with a gun in his hand. Angeli told some cock-and-bull story about expecting a burglar. My guess is that Dr Hadley's arrival saved Stevens's life.'

'How did you first get on to Angeli?' Sullivan asked.

'It started with a couple of tips that he was shaking down some merchants,' McGreavy said. 'When I went to check them out, the victims wouldn't talk. They were scared, but I couldn't figure out why. I didn't say anything to Angeli. I just started keeping a close watch on him. When the Hanson murder broke, Angeli came and asked if he could work on the case with me. He gave me some bullshit about how much he admired me and how he had always wanted to be my partner. I knew he had to have an angle, so with Captain Bertelli's permission, I played along with him. No wonder he wanted to work on the case – he was in it up to his ass! At that time I wasn't sure whether Dr Stevens was involved in the murders of Hanson and Carol Roberts, but I decided to use him to set up Angeli. I built up a phoney case against Stevens and told Angeli I was going to nail the doctor for the murders. I figured that if Angeli thought he was off the hook, he'd relax and get careless.'

'Did it work?'

'No. Angeli surprised the hell out of me by putting up a fight to keep Stevens out of jail.'

Sullivan looked up, puzzled. 'But why?'

'Because he was trying to knock him off and he couldn't get to him if he were locked up.'

'When McGreavy began to put the pressure on,' Captain Bertelli said, 'Angeli came to me hinting that McGreavy was trying to frame Dr Stevens.'

'We were sure then that we were on the right track,' McGreavy said. 'Stevens hired a private detective named Norman Moody. I checked Moody out and learned that he had tangled with Angeli before when a client of Moody's was picked up by Angeli on a drugs rap. Moody said his client was framed. Knowing what I know now, I'd say Moody was telling the truth.'

'So Moody lucked into the answer from the beginning.'

'It wasn't all luck. Moody was bright. He knew Angeli was probably involved. When he found the bomb in Dr Stevens's car, he turned it over to the FBI and asked them to check it out.'

'He was afraid if Angeli got hold of it, he'd find a way to get rid of it?'

'That's my guess. But someone slipped up and a copy of the report was sent to Angeli. He knew then that Moody was on to him. The real break we got was when Moody came up with the name "Don Vinton".'

'Cosa Nostra for "The Big Man".'

'Yeah. For some reason, someone in La Cosa Nostra was out to get Dr Stevens.'

'How did you tie up Angeli with La Cosa Nostra?'

'I went back to the merchants Angeli had been putting the squeeze on. When I mentioned La Cosa

Nostra, they panicked. Angeli was working for one of the Cosa Nostra families, but he got greedy and was doing a little shake-down business of his own on the side.'

'Why would La Cosa Nostra want to kill Dr Stevens?' Sullivan asked.

'I don't know. We're working on several angles.' He sighed wearily. 'We got two lousy breaks. Angeli slipped the men we had tailing him, and Dr Stevens ran away from the hospital before I could warn him about Angeli and give him protection.'

The switchboard flashed. An operator plugged in the call and listened a moment. 'Captain Bertelli.'

Bertelli grabbed the extension phone. 'Captain Bertelli.' He listened, saying nothing, then slowly replaced the receiver and turned to McGreavy. 'They lost them.'

Chapter Twenty-two

Anthony DeMarco had mana.

Judd could feel the burning power of his personality across the room, coming in waves that struck like a tangible force. When Anne had said her husband was handsome, she had not exaggerated.

DeMarco had a classic Roman face with a perfectly sculptured profile, coal black eyes, and attractive streaks of grey in his dark hair. He was in his middle forties, tall and athletic, and moved with a restless animal grace. His voice was deep and magnetic. 'Would you care for a drink, Doctor?'

Judd shook his head, fascinated by the man before him. Anyone would have sworn that DeMarco was a perfectly normal, charming man, a perfect host welcoming an honoured guest.

There were five of them in the richly panelled library. Judd, DeMarco, Detective Angeli, and the two men who had tried to kill Judd at his apartment building, Rocky and Nick Vaccaro. They had formed a circle around Judd. He was looking into the faces of the enemy, and there was a grim satisfaction in it. Finally he knew who he was fighting. If 'fighting' was the right word. He had walked into Angeli's trap. Worse. He had phoned Angeli and invited him to come and get him! Angeli, the Judas goat who had led him here to the slaughter.

DeMarco was studying him with deep interest, his black eyes probing. 'I've heard a great deal about you,' he said.

Judd said nothing.

'Forgive me for having you brought here in this fashion, but it is necessary to ask you a few questions.' He smiled apologetically, radiating warmth.

Judd knew what was coming, and his mind moved swiftly ahead.

'What did you and my wife talk about, Dr Stevens?'

Judd put surprise into his voice. 'Your wife? I don't know your wife.'

DeMarco shook his head reproachfully. 'She's been going to your office twice a week for the last three weeks.'

Judd frowned thoughtfully. 'I have no patient named DeMarco . . .'

De Marco nodded understandingly. 'Perhaps she used another name. Maybe her maiden name. Blake – Anne Blake.'

Judd carefully registered surprise. 'Anne Blake?'

The two Vaccaro brothers moved in closer.

'No,' DeMarco said sharply. He turned to Judd. His affable manner was gone. 'Doctor, if you try to play games with me, I'm going to do things to you that you wouldn't believe.'

Judd looked into his eyes and believed him. He knew that his life was hanging by a thread. He forced indignation into his voice. 'You can do what you please. Until this moment I had no idea that Anne Blake was your wife.'

'That could be true,' Angeli said. 'He – '

DeMarco ignored Angeli. 'What did you and my wife talk about for three weeks?'

They had arrived at the moment of truth. From the instant Judd had seen the bronze rooster on the roof, the final pieces of the puzzle had fallen into place. Anne had not set him up for murder. She had been a victim, like himself. She had married Anthony DeMarco, successful owner of a large construction firm, without any idea of who he really was. Then something must have happened to make her suspect that her husband was not what he had seemed to be, that he was involved in something dark and terrible. With no one to talk to, she had turned for help to an analyst, a stranger, in whom she could confide. But in Judd's office her basic loyalty to her husband had kept her from discussing her fears.

'We didn't talk about much of anything,' said Judd evenly. 'Your wife refused to tell me what her problem was.'

DeMarco's black eyes were fixed on him, probing, weighing. 'You'll have to come up with something better than that.'

How DeMarco must have panicked when he learned that his wife was going to a psychoanalyst – the wife of a leader in La Cosa Nostra. No wonder DeMarco had killed, trying to get hold of Anne's file.

'All she told me,' Judd said, 'was that she was unhappy about something, but couldn't discuss it.'

'That took ten seconds,' DeMarco said. 'I've got a record of every minute she spent in your office. What did she talk about for the rest of the three weeks? She must have told you who I am.'

'She said you owned a construction company.'

DeMarco was studying him coldly. Judd could feel beads of perspiration forming on his forehead.

'I've been reading up on analysis, Doctor. The patient talks about everything that's on his mind.'

'That's part of the therapy,' Judd said matter-of-factly. 'That's why I wasn't getting anywhere with Mrs Blake – with Mrs DeMarco. I intended to dismiss her as a patient.'

'But you didn't.'

'I didn't have to. When she came to see me Friday, she told me that she was leaving for Europe.'

'Annie's changed her mind. She doesn't want to go to Europe with me. Do you know why?'

Judd looked at him, genuinely puzzled. 'No.'

'Because of you, Doctor.'

Judd's heart gave a little leap. He carefully kept his feelings out of his voice. 'I don't understand.'

'Sure you do. Annie and I had a long talk last night. She thinks she made a mistake about our marriage. She's not happy with me anymore, because she thinks she goes for you.' When DeMarco spoke, it was almost in a hypnotic whisper. 'I want you to tell me all about what happened when you two were alone in your office and she was on your couch.'

Judd steeled himself against the mixed emotions that were coursing through him. She *did* care! But what good was it going to do either of them? DeMarco was looking at him, waiting for an answer. 'Nothing happened. If you read up on analysis, you'll know that every female patient goes through an emotional transference. At one time or another, they all think they're in love with their doctor. It's just a passing phase.'

210

DeMarco was watching him intently, his black eyes probing into Judd's.

'How did you know she was coming to see me?' Judd asked, making the question casual.

DeMarco looked at Judd a moment, then walked over to a large desk and picked up a razor-sharp letter opener in the shape of a dagger. 'One of my men saw her go into your building. There are a lot of baby doctors there and they figured maybe Annie was keeping back a little surprise from me. They followed her up to your office.' He turned to Judd.

'It was a surprise, all right. They found out she was going to a psychiatrist. The wife of Anthony DeMarco spilling my personal business to a headshrinker.'

'I told you she didn't – '

DeMarco's voice was soft. 'The *Commissione* held a meeting. They voted for me to kill her, like we'd kill any traitor.' He was pacing now, reminding Judd of a dangerous, caged animal. 'But they can't give me orders like a peasant soldier. I am Anthony DeMarco, a Capo. I promised them that if she had discussed any of our business, I would kill the man she talked to. With these two hands.' He held up his fists, one of them holding the razor-edged dagger. 'That's you, Doctor.'

DeMarco was circling him now as he talked, and each time that DeMarco walked in back of him, Judd unconsciously braced himself.

'You're making a mistake if – ' Judd started.

'No. You know who made the mistake? Annie.' He looked Judd up and down. He sounded genuinely puzzled. 'How could she think you're a better man than I am?'

211

The Vaccaro brothers snickered.

'You're nothing. A patsy who goes to an office every day and makes – what? Thirty grand a year? Fifty? A hundred? I make more than that in a week.' DeMarco's mask was slipping away more quickly now, eroding under the pressure of his emotions. He was beginning to speak in short, excited bursts, a patina of ugliness warping his handsome features. Anne had only seen him behind his façade. Judd was looking into the naked face of a homicidal paranoiac. 'You and that little *putana* pick each other!'

'We haven't picked each other,' Judd said.

DeMarco was watching him, his eyes blazing. 'She doesn't mean anything to you?'

'I told you. She's just another patient.'

'Okay,' DeMarco said at last. 'You tell her.'

'Tell her what?'

'That you don't give a damn about her. I'm going to send her down here. I want you to talk to her, alone.'

Judd's pulse began to race. He was going to be given a chance to save himself and Anne.

DeMarco flicked his hand and the men moved out into the hallway. DeMarco turned to Judd. His deep black eyes were hooded. He smiled gently, the mask in place again. 'As long as Annie doesn't know anything, she will live. You're going to convince her that she should go to Europe with me.'

Judd felt his mouth go suddenly dry. There was a triumphant glint in DeMarco's eyes. Judd knew why. He had underestimated his opponent.

Fatally.

DeMarco was not a chess player, and yet he had been

212

clever enough to know that he held a pawn that made Judd helpless. Anne. Whatever move Judd made, she was in danger. If he sent her away to Europe with DeMarco, he was certain that her life would be in jeopardy. He did not believe that DeMarco was going to let her live. La Cosa Nostra would not allow it. In Europe DeMarco would arrange an 'accident'. But if Judd told Anne not to go, if she found out what was happening to him, she would try to interfere, and that would mean instant death for her. There was no escape: only a choice of two traps.

From the window of her bedroom on the second floor, Anne had watched the arrival of Judd and Angeli. For one exhilarating moment, she had believed that Judd was coming to take her away, to rescue her from the terrifying situation she was in. But then she had seen Angeli take out a gun and force Judd into the house.

She had known the truth about her husband for the last forty-eight hours. Before that, it had only been a dim, glimmering suspicion, so incredible that she had tried to brush it aside. It had begun a few months ago, when she had gone to a play in Manhattan and had come home unexpectedly early because the star was drunk and the curtain had been rung down in the middle of the second act. Anthony had told her that he was having a business meeting at the house, but that it would be over before she returned. When she had arrived, the meeting was still going on. And before her surprised husband had been able to close the library door, she had heard someone angrily shouting, 'I vote that we hit the factory tonight and take care of the bastards once and for all!' The phrase, the ruthless appearance of the strangers in the room, and Anthony's agitation at seeing her combined to unnerve Anne. She had let his glib explanations convince her because she had wanted desperately to be convinced. In the six months of their marriage, he had been a tender, considerate husband. She had seen occasional flashes of a violent temper, but he had always quickly managed to gain control of himself.

A few weeks after the theatre incident, she had picked up a telephone and had overheard Anthony's voice on an extension phone. 'We're taking over a shipment from Toronto tonight. You'll have to have someone handle the guard. He's not with us.'

She had hung up, shaken. 'Take over a shipment' . . . 'handle the guard' . . . They sounded ominous, but they could have been innocent business phrases. Carefully, casually, she tried to question Anthony about his business activities. It was as though a steel wall went up. She was confronted by an angry stranger who told her to take care of his home and keep out of his business. They had quarrelled bitterly, and the next evening he had given her an outrageously expensive necklace and tenderly apologized.

A month later, the third incident had occurred. Anne had been awakened at four o'clock in the morning by the slamming of a door. She had slipped into a negligee and gone downstairs to investigate. She heard voices coming from the library, raised in argument. She went towards the door, but stopped as she saw Anthony in the room talking to half a dozen strangers. Afraid that he would be angry if she interrupted, she quietly went back upstairs and returned to bed. At breakfast the next morning, she asked him how he had slept.

'Great. I fell off at ten o'clock and never opened my eyes once.'

And Anne knew that she was in trouble. She had no idea what kind of trouble or how serious it was. All she knew was that her husband had lied to her for reasons that she could not fathom. What kind of business could he be involved in that had to be conducted secretly in the middle of the night with men who looked like hoodlums? She was afraid to broach the subject again with Anthony. A panic began to build in her. There was no one with whom she could talk.

A few nights later, at a dinner party at the country club to which they belonged, someone had mentioned a psychoanalyst named Judd Stevens, and talked about how brilliant he was.

'He's a kind of analyst's analyst, if you know what I mean. He's terribly attractive, but it's wasted – he's one of those dedicated types.'

Anne had carefully noted the name and the following week had gone to see him.

The first meeting with Judd had turned her life topsy-turvy. She had felt herself drawn into an emotional vortex that had left her shaken. In her confusion, she had been scarcely able to talk to him, and she had left feeling like a schoolgirl, promising herself that she would not go back. But she had gone back to prove to herself that what had happened was a fluke, an accident. Her reaction the second time was even stronger. She had always prided herself on being sensible and realistic, and now she was acting like a seventeen-year-old girl in love for the first time. She found herself unable to discuss her husband with Judd, and so they had talked about other things, and after each session Anne found herself more in love with this warm, sensitive stranger.

She knew it was hopeless because she would never divorce Anthony. She felt there must be some terrible flaw in her that would allow her to marry a man and six months later fall in love with another man. She decided that it would be better if she never saw Judd again.

And then a series of strange things had begun to happen. Carol Roberts was killed, and Judd was knocked down by a hit-and-run driver. She read in the newspapers that Judd was there when Moody's body was found in the Five Star Warehouse. She had seen the name of the warehouse before.

On the letterhead of an invoice on Anthony's desk.

And a terrible suspicion began to form in her mind.

It seemed incredible that Anthony could be involved in any of the awful things that had been happening, and yet . . . She felt as though she was trapped in a terrifying nightmare, and there was no way out. She could not discuss her fears with Judd, and she was afraid to discuss them with Anthony. She told herself that her suspicions were groundless: Anthony did not even know of Judd's existence.

And then, forty-eight hours ago, Anthony had come into her bedroom and started questioning her about her visits to Judd. Her first reaction had been anger that he had been spying on her, but that had quickly given way to all the fears that had been preying upon her. As she looked into his twisted, enraged face, she knew that her husband was capable of anything.

Even murder.

During the questioning, she had made one terrible mistake. She had let him know how she felt about Judd. Anthony's eyes had turned deep black, and he had shaken his head as though warding off a physical blow.

It was not until she was alone again that she realized how much danger Judd was in, and that she could not leave him. She told Anthony that she would not go to Europe with him.

And now Judd was here, in this house. His life in peril, because of her.

The bedroom door opened and Anthony walked in. He stood watching her for a moment.

'You have a visitor,' he said.

She walked into the library wearing a yellow skirt and blouse, her hair back loosely over her shoulders. Her face was drawn and pale, but there was an air of quiet composure about her. Judd was in the room, alone.

'Hello, Dr Stevens. Anthony told me that you were here.'

Judd had the sensation that they were acting out a charade for the benefit of an unseen, deadly audience. He intuitively knew that Anne was aware of the situation and was placing herself in his hands, waiting to follow whatever lead he offered.

And there was nothing he could do except try to keep her alive a little longer. If Anne refused to go to Europe, DeMarco would certainly have her killed here.

He hesitated, choosing his words carefully. Each word could be as dangerous as the bomb planted in his car. 'Mrs DeMarco, your husband is upset because you changed your mind about going to Europe with him.'

Anne waited, listening, weighing.

'I'm sorry,' she said.

'So am I. I think you should go,' Judd said, raising his voice.

Anne was studying his face, reading his eyes. 'What if I refuse? What if I just walk out?'

Judd was filled with sudden alarm. 'You mustn't do that.' She would never leave this house alive. 'Mrs DeMarco,' he said deliberately, 'your husband is under the mistaken impression that you're in love with me.'

She opened her lips to speak and he quickly went on, 'I explained to him that that's a normal part of analysis – an emotional transference that all patients go through.'

She picked up his lead. 'I know. I'm afraid it was foolish of me to go to you in the first place. I should have tried to solve my problem myself.' Her eyes told him how much she meant it, how much she regretted the danger she had placed him in. 'I've been thinking it over. Perhaps a holiday in Europe would be good for me.'

He breathed a quick sigh of relief. She had understood.

But there was no way he could warn her of the real danger. Or did she know? And even if she knew, was there anything she could do about it? He looked past Anne towards the library window framing the tall trees that bordered the woods. She had told him that she took long walks in them. It was possible she might be familiar with a way out. If they could get to the woods . . . He lowered his voice, urgently. 'Anne – '

'Finished your little chat?'

Judd spun around. DeMarco had quietly walked into the room. Behind him came Angeli and the Vaccaro brothers.

Anne turned to her husband. 'Yes,' she said. 'Dr Stevens thinks I should go to Europe with you. I'm going to take his advice.'

DeMarco smiled and looked at Judd. 'I knew I could count on you, Doctor.' He was radiating charm, beaming with the expansive satisfaction of a man who has achieved total victory. It was as though the incredible energy that flowed through DeMarco could be converted at will, switched from a dark evil to an overpowering, attractive warmth. No wonder Anne had been taken in by him. Even Judd found it hard to believe at this instant that this gracious, friendly Adonis was a cold-blooded, psychopathic murderer.

DeMarco turned to Anne. 'We'll be leaving early in the morning, darling. Why don't you go upstairs and start packing?'

Anne hesitated. She did not want to leave Judd alone with these men. 'I . . .' She looked at Judd helplessly. He nodded imperceptibly.

'All right.' Anne held out her hand. 'Goodbye, Dr Stevens.'

Judd took her hand. 'Goodbye.'

And this time it *was* goodbye. There was no way out. Judd watched as she turned, nodded at the others, and walked out of the room.

DeMarco looked after her. 'Isn't she beautiful?' There was a strange expression on his face. Love, possessiveness – and something else. Regret? For what he was about to do to Anne?

'She doesn't know anything about all this,' Judd said. 'Why don't you keep her out of it? Let her go away.'

He watched the switch turn in DeMarco, and it was almost physical. The charm vanished, and hate began to fill the room, a current flowing from DeMarco to Judd, not touching anyone else. There was an ecstatic, almost orgiastic expression on DeMarco's face. 'Let's go, Doctor.'

Judd looked around the room, measuring his chances of escape. Surely DeMarco would prefer not to kill him in his home. It had to be now or never. The Vaccaro brothers were watching him hungrily, hoping he would make a move. Angeli was standing near the window, his hand near his gun holster. 'I wouldn't try it,' DeMarco said softly. 'You're a dead man – but we're going to do it my way.'

He gave Judd a push towards the door. The others closed in on him, and they headed towards the entrance hall.

When Anne reached the upstairs hallway, she waited near the landing, watching the hall below. She drew back out of sight as she saw Judd and the others move towards the front door. She hurried into her bedroom and looked out the window. The men were pushing Judd into Angeli's car.

Quickly Anne reached for the telephone and dialled operator. It seemed an eternity before there was an answer.

'Operator, I want the police! Hurry – it's an emergency!'

And a man's hand reached in front of her and

pressed down the receiver. Anne gave a little scream and whirled around. Nick Vaccaro was standing over her, grinning.

Chapter Twenty-three

Angeli switched on the headlights. It was four o'clock in the afternoon, but the sun was buried somewhere behind the mass of cumulus clouds that scudded overhead, pushed by the icy winds. They had been driving for over an hour.

Angeli was at the wheel. Rocky Vaccaro was seated next to him. Judd was in the back seat with Anthony DeMarco.

In the beginning Judd had kept an eye out for a passing police car, hoping that he might somehow make a desperate bid to attract attention, but Angeli was driving through little-used side roads where there was almost no traffic. They skirted the edges of Morristown, picked up Route 206 and headed south towards the sparsely populated, bleak plains of central New Jersey. The grey sky opened up and it began to pour: a cold, icy sleet that beat against the windscreen like tiny drums gone mad.

'Slow down,' DeMarco commanded. 'We don't want to have an accident.'

Angeli obediently lightened his foot on the accelerator.

DeMarco turned to Judd. 'That's where most people make their mistake. They don't plan things out like me.'

Judd looked at DeMarco, studying him clinically.

The man was suffering from megalomania, beyond the reach of reason or logic. There was no way to appeal to him. There was some moral sense missing in him that allowed him to kill without compunction. Judd knew most of the answers now.

DeMarco had committed the murders with his own hand out of a sense of honour – a Sicilian's revenge, to erase the stain that he thought his wife had placed on him and his Cosa Nostra family. He had killed John Hanson by mistake. When Angeli had reported back to him and told him what had happened, DeMarco had gone back to the office and found Carol. Poor Carol. She could not give him the tapes of Mrs DeMarco because she did not know Anne by that name. If DeMarco had kept his temper, he could have helped Carol figure out whom he was talking about; but it was part of his sickness that he had no tolerance for frustration and he had gone into an insane rage, and Carol had died. Horribly. It was DeMarco who had run Judd down, and later had come to kill him at his office with Angeli. Judd had been puzzled by the fact that they had not broken in and shot him. But he realized now that since McGreavy was sure Judd was guilty, they had decided to make his death look like a suicide, committed in remorse. That would stop any further police investigation.

And Moody . . . poor Moody. When Judd had told him the names of the detectives on the case, he had thought he was reacting to McGreavy – when it was really Angeli. Moody had learned that Angeli was involved with the Cosa Nostra, and when he followed up on it . . .

He looked over at DeMarco. 'What's going to happen to Anne?'

'Don't worry. I'll take care of her,' DeMarco said.

Angeli smiled. 'Yeah.'

Judd felt a helpless rage sweep over him.

'I was wrong to marry someone outside the family,' brooded DeMarco. 'Outsiders can never understand it like it is. Never.'

They were travelling in an almost barren section of flatlands. An occasional factory dotted the sleet-blurred skyline in the distance.

'We're almost there,' Angeli announced.

'You've done a good job,' DeMarco said. 'We're going to hide you away somewhere until the heat cools down. Where would you like to go?'

'I like Florida.'

DeMarco nodded approvingly. 'No problem. You'll stay with one of the *family*.'

'I know some great broads down there.' Angeli smiled.

DeMarco smiled back at him in the mirror. 'You'll come back with a tanned ass.'

'I hope that's all I come back with.'

Rocky Vaccaro laughed.

In the distance, on the right, Judd saw the sprawled buildings of a factory spuming smoke into the air. They reached a small side road leading to the factory. Angeli turned into it and drove until they came to a high wall. The gate was closed. Angeli leaned on the horn and a man in a raincoat and rain hat appeared behind the gate. When he saw DeMarco, he nodded, unlocked the gate, and swung it open. Angeli drove the car inside, and the gate closed behind them. They had arrived.

At the Nineteenth Precinct, Lieutenant McGreavy was in his office, going over a list of names with three detectives, Captain Bertelli, and the two FBI men.

'This is a list of the Cosa Nostra families in the East. All the Sub-Capos and Capo Regimes. Our problem is, we don't know which one Angeli is hooked up with.'

'How long would it take to get a rundown on them?' asked Bertelli.

One of the FBI men spoke. 'There are over sixty names here. It would take at least twenty-four hours, but . . .' He stopped.

McGreavy finished the sentence for him. 'But Dr Stevens won't be alive in twenty-four hours from now.'

A young uniformed policeman hurried up to the open door. He hesitated as he saw the group of men.

'What is it?' McGreavy asked.

'New Jersey didn't know if it's important, Lieutenant, but you asked them to report anything unusual. An operator got a call from an adult female asking for Police Headquarters. She said it was an emergency, and then the line went dead. The operator waited, but there was no call back.'

'Where did the call come from?'

'A town called Old Tappan.'

'Did she get the number?'

'No. The caller hung up too quickly.'

'Great,' McGreavy said bitterly.

'Forget it,' Bertelli said. 'It was probably some old lady reporting a lost cat.'

McGreavy's phone rang, a long, insistent peal. He picked up the phone. 'Lieutenant McGreavy.' The others in the room watched his face draw tight with tension. 'Right! Tell them not to make a move until I get there. I'm on my way!' He slammed the receiver down. 'The Highway Patrol just spotted Angeli's car going south on Route 206, just outside Millstone.'

'Are they tailing it?' It was one of the FBI men.

'The patrol car was going in the opposite direction. By the time they got turned around, it had disappeared. I know that area. There's nothing out there but a few factories.' He turned to one of the FBI men. 'Can you get me a fast rundown on the names of the factories there and who owns them?'

'Will do.' The FBI man reached for the phone.

'I'm heading out there,' McGreavy said. 'Call me when you get it.' He turned to the men. 'Let's move!' He started out the door, the three detectives and the second FBI man on his heels.

Angeli drove past the watchman's shack near the gate and continued towards a group of odd-looking structures that reached into the sky. There were high brick chimneys and giant flumes, their curved shapes rearing up out of the grey drizzle like prehistoric monsters in an ancient, timeless landscape.

The car rolled up to a complex of large pipes and conveyor belts and braked to a stop. Angeli and Vaccaro got out of the car and Vaccaro opened the rear door on Judd's side. He had a gun in his hand. 'Out, Doctor.'

Slowly, Judd got out of the car, followed by DeMarco. A tremendous din and wind hurtled at them.

In front of them, about twenty-five feet away, was an enormous pipeline filled with roaring, compressed air, sucking in everything that came near its open, greedy lip.

'This is one of the biggest pipelines in the country,' DeMarco boasted, raising his voice to make himself heard. 'Do you want to see how it works?'

Judd looked at him incredulously. DeMarco was acting the part of the perfect host again, entertaining a guest. No – not acting. He *meant* it. That was what was terrifying. DeMarco was about to murder Judd, and it would be a routine business transaction, something that had to be taken care of, like disposing of a piece of useless equipment, but he wanted to impress him first.

'Come on, Doctor. It's interesting.'

They moved towards the pipeline, Angeli leading the way. DeMarco at Judd's side and Rocky Vaccaro bringing up the rear.

'This plant grosses over five million dollars a year,' DeMarco said proudly. 'The whole operation is automatic.'

As they got closer to the pipeline, the roar increased, the noise became almost intolerable. A hundred yards from the entrance to the vacuum chamber, a large conveyor belt carried giant logs to a planing machine twenty feet long and five feet high, with half a dozen razor-sharp cutter heads. The planed logs were then carried upwards to a hog, a fierce porcupine-looking rotor bristling with knives. The air was filled with flying sawdust mixed with rain, being sucked into the pipeline.

'It doesn't matter how big the logs are,' DeMarco said proudly. 'The machines cut them down to fit that thirty-six-inch pipe.'

DeMarco took a snub-nosed .38 Colt out of his pocket and called out, 'Angeli.'

Angeli turned.

'Have a good trip to Florida.' DeMarco squeezed the trigger, and a red hole exploded in Angeli's shirt front. Angeli stared at DeMarco with a puzzled half-smile on his face, as though waiting for the answer to a riddle he had just heard. DeMarco pulled the trigger again. Angeli crumpled to the ground. DeMarco nodded to Rocky Vaccaro, and the big man picked up Angeli's body, slung it over his shoulder, and moved towards the pipeline.

DeMarco turned to Judd. 'Angeli was stupid. Every cop in the country's looking for him. If they found him, he'd lead them to me.'

The cold-blooded murder of Angeli was shock enough, but what followed was even worse. Judd watched, horrified, as Vaccaro carried Angeli's body towards the lip of the giant pipeline. The tremendous pressure caught at Angeli's body, greedily sucking it in. Vaccaro had to grab a large metal handle on the lip of the pipe to keep himself from being pulled in by the deadly cyclone of air. Judd had one last glimpse of Angeli's body whirling into the pipe through the vortex of sawdust and logs, and it was gone. Vaccaro reached for the valve next to the lip of the pipe and turned it. A cover slid over the mouth of the pipe, shutting off the cyclone of air. Then the sudden silence was deafening.

DeMarco turned to Judd and raised his gun. There was an exalted, mystic expression on his face, and Judd realized that murder was almost a religious experience for him. It was a crucible that purified. Judd knew that his moment of death had come. He felt no fear for himself, but he was consumed by rage that this man would be allowed to live, to murder Anne, to destroy other innocent, decent people. He heard a growling, a moan of rage and frustration, and realized it was coming from his own lips. He was like a trapped animal obsessed with the desire to kill his captor.

DeMarco was smiling at him, reading his thoughts. 'I'm going to give it to you in the gut, Doctor. It'll take a little longer, but you'll have more time to worry about what's going to happen to Annie.'

There was one hope. One slim hope.

'Someone should worry about her,' Judd said. 'She's never had a man.'

DeMarco stared at him blankly.

Judd was yelling now, fighting to make DeMarco listen. 'Do you know what your cock is? That gun in your hand. Without a gun or a knife, you're a woman.'

He saw DeMarco's face fill with slow rage.

'You have no balls, DeMarco. Without that gun, you're a joke.'

A red film was filling DeMarco's eyes, like a warning flag of death. Vaccaro took a step forward. DeMarco waved him back.

'I'll kill you with these bare hands,' DeMarco said as he threw the gun to the ground. 'With these bare hands!' Slowly, like a powerful animal, he started towards Judd.

Judd backed away, out of reach. He knew he stood no chance against DeMarco physically. His only hope was to work on DeMarco's sick mind, making it unable to function. He had to keep striking at DeMarco's most vulnerable area – his pride in his manhood. 'You're a homosexual, DeMarco!'

DeMarco laughed and lunged at him. Judd moved out of reach.

Vaccaro picked up the gun from the ground. 'Chief! Let me finish him!'

'Keep out of this!' DeMarco roared.

The two men circled, feinting for position. Judd's foot slipped on a pile of soggy sawdust, and DeMarco rushed at him like a charging bull. His huge fist hit Judd on the side of the mouth, knocking him back. Judd recovered and lashed out at DeMarco, hitting him in the face. DeMarco rocked back, then lunged forward and drove his fists into Judd's stomach. Three smashing blows that knocked the breath out of Judd. He tried to speak to taunt DeMarco, but he was gasping for air. DeMarco was hovering over him like a savage bird of prey.

'Getting winded, Doctor?' he laughed. 'I was a boxer. I'm going to give you lessons. I'm going to work on your kidneys and then your head and your eyes. I'm gonna put your eyes out, Doctor. Before I'm through with you, you're going to beg me to shoot you.'

Judd believed him. In the eerie light that spilled from the clouded sky, DeMarco looked like an enraged animal. He rushed at Judd again and caught him with his fist, splitting his cheek open with a heavy cameo ring. Judd lashed out at DeMarco, pounding at his face with both fists. DeMarco did not even flinch.

DeMarco began hitting Judd's kidneys, his hands working like pistons. Judd pulled away, his body a sea of pain.

'You're not getting tired, are you, Doctor?' He started to close in again. Judd knew that his body could not take much more punishment. He had to keep talking. It was his only chance.

'DeMarco . . .' He gasped.

DeMarco feinted and Judd swung at him. DeMarco ducked, laughed, and slammed his fist squarely between Judd's legs. Judd doubled over, filled with an unbelievable agony, and fell to the ground. DeMarco was on top of him, his hands at his throat.

'My bare hands,' DeMarco screamed. 'I'm going to tear your eyes out with my bare hands.' He dug his huge fists into Judd's eyes.

They were speeding past Bedminster heading south on Route 206, when the call cracked in over the radio. 'Code Three . . . Code Three . . . All cars stand by . . . New York Unit Twenty-seven . . . New York Unit Twenty-seven . . .'

McGreavy grabbed the radio microphone. 'New York Twenty-seven . . . Come in!'

Captain Bertelli's excited voice came over the radio. 'We've got it pinned down, Mac. There's a New Jersey pipeline company two miles south of Millstone. It's owned by the Five Star Corporation – the same company that owns the meat-packing plant. It's one of the fronts Tony DeMarco uses.'

'Sounds right,' McGreavy said. 'We're on our way.'

'How far are you from there?'

'Ten miles.'

'Good luck.'

'Yeah.'

McGreavy switched off the radio, hit the siren, and slammed the accelerator to the floorboard.

*

231

The sky was spinning in wet circles overhead and something was pounding at him, tearing his body apart. He tried to see, but his eyes were swollen shut. A fist smashed into his ribs, and he felt the agonizing splinter of bones breaking. He could feel DeMarco's hot breath on his face, coming in quick excited gasps. He tried to see him, but he was locked in darkness. He opened his mouth and forced words past his thick, swollen tongue. 'You s-see,' he gasped. 'I was r-right . . . You can – you can only hit a man – when he's down . . .'

The breathing in his face stopped. He felt two hands grab him and pull him to his feet.

'You're a dead man, Doctor. And I did it with my bare hands.'

Judd backed away from the voice. 'You're an – an a-animal,' he said, gasping for breath. 'psychopath . . . You should be locked up . . . in an . . . insane asylum.'

DeMarco's voice was thick with rage. 'You're a liar!'

'It's the t-truth,' Judd said, moving back. 'Your . . . your brain is diseased . . . Your mind is going to . . . snap and you'll be . . . like an idiot baby.' Judd backed away, unable to see where he was going. Behind him he heard the faint hum of the closed pipeline, waiting like a sleeping giant.

DeMarco lunged at Judd, his huge hands clutching his throat. 'I'm going to break your neck!' His enormous fingers closed on Judd's windpipe, squeezing.

Judd felt his head begin to swim. This was his last chance. Every instinct in him screamed out to grab DeMarco's hands and pull them away from his throat so that he could breathe. Instead, with a final tremendous effort of will, he put his hands in back of him, fumbling for the pipe valve. He felt himself beginning to slide into unconsciousness, and in that instant his hands closed on the valve. With a final, desperate burst of energy, he turned the handle and swerved his body around so that DeMarco was nearest the opening. A tremendous vacuum of air suddenly blasted at them, trying to pull them into the vortex of the pipe. Judd clung frantically to the valve with both hands, fighting the cyclonic fury of the wind. He felt DeMarco's fingers digging into his throat as DeMarco was pulled towards the pipe. DeMarco could have saved himself, but in his mindless insane fury, he refused to let go. Judd could not see DeMarco's face, but the voice was a demented animal cry, the words lost in the roar of the wind.

Judd's fingers started to slip off the valve. He was going to be pulled into the pipeline with DeMarco. He gave a quick, last prayer, and in that instant he felt DeMarco's hands slip away from his throat. There was a loud, reverberating scream, and then only the roar from the pipeline. DeMarco had vanished.

Judd stood there, bone weary, unable to move, waiting for the shot from Vaccaro.

A moment later it rang out.

He stood there, wondering why Vaccaro had missed. Through the dull haze of pain, he heard more shots, and the sound of feet running, and then his name being called. And then someone had an arm around him and McGreavy's voice was saying, 'Mother of God! Look at his face!'

Strong hands gripped his arm and pulled him away from the awful roaring tug of the pipeline. Something wet was running down his cheeks and he did not know whether it was blood or tears, and he did not care.

It was over.

He forced one puffed eye open and through a narrow, blood-red slit, he could dimly see McGreavy. 'Anne's at the house,' Judd said. 'DeMarco's wife. We've got to go to her.'

McGreavy was looking at him strangely, not moving, and Judd realized that no words had come out. He lifted his mouth up to McGreavy's ear and spoke slowly, in a hoarse, broken croak. 'Anne DeMarco . . . She's at the . . . house . . . help.'

McGreavy walked over to the police car, picked up the radio transmitter, and issued instructions. Judd stood there, unsteady, still rocking back and forth from DeMarco's blows, letting the cold, biting wind wash over him. In front of him he could see a body lying on the ground, and knew it was Rocky Vaccaro.

We've won, he thought. *We've won.* He kept saying the phrase over and over in his mind. And even as he said it, he knew it was meaningless. What kind of victory was it? He had thought of himself as a decent, civilized human being – a doctor, a healer – and he had turned into a savage animal filled with the lust to kill. He had sent a sick man over the brink of insanity and then murdered him. It was a terrible burden he would have to live with always. Because even though he could tell himself it was in self-defence, he knew – God help him – that he had enjoyed doing it. And for that he could never forgive himself. He was no better than DeMarco, or the Vaccaro brothers, or any of the others. Civilization was a thin, dangerously fragile veneer, and when that veneer cracked, man became one of the beasts again, falling back into the slime of the primeval abyss he prided himself on having climbed up from.

Judd was too weary to think about it any longer. Now he wanted only to see that Anne was safe.

McGreavy was standing there, his manner strangely gentle.

'There's a police car on the way to her house, Dr Stevens. Okay?'

Judd nodded gratefully.

McGreavy took his arm and guided him towards a car. As he moved slowly, painfully, across the court-yard, he realized that it had stopped raining. On the far horizon the thunderheads had been swept away by the raw December wind, and the sky was clearing. In the west a small ray of light appeared as the sun began to fight its way through, growing brighter and brighter.

It was going to be a beautiful Christmas.

The Doomsday Conspiracy
Sidney Sheldon

A devastatingly topical novel from
the world's master storyteller

Robert Bellamy of US naval intelligence, a disillusioned man
recovering from a broken marriage, is despatched on a top
secret mission. A weather balloon, he is told, carrying
sensitive military information, has crashed in Switzerland
and Bellamy must locate the ten witnesses to the incident.
But when he arrives in Switzerland he discovers that it wasn't
a weather balloon that crashed after all, but a UFO with two
dead aliens aboard, whose remains have since vanished . . .
As the story unfolds, Bellamy gradually discovers the full,
terrible nature of Operation Doomsday, a conspiracy of such
magnitude as to threaten the destruction of the earth's
environment. He also rebuilds his own shattered life, finding
true love and hope for the future again.

ISBN 0 00 647208 7

The Other Side of Midnight
Sidney Sheldon

The magnificent novel of scorching sensation and shimmering evil that became a triumphant screen sensation.

A beautiful French actress whose craving for passion and vengeance took her from the gutters of Paris to the bedroom of a millionaire . . . a dynamic Greek tycoon who never forgot an insult, never forgave an injury . . . a handsome war hero drawn from his wife to a woman none could resist . . . and a girl whose dream of love was transformed into a nightmare of fear . . .

Paris and Washington, Hollywood and the islands of Greece are the settings for a dramatic narrative of four star-crossed lives enmeshed in a deadly ritual of passion, intrigue and corruption where the punishment will always exceed the crime . . .

'Gripping, glamorous, memorable, heart-stopping.'

Irving Wallace

ISBN 0 00 617931 2

Nothing Lasts Forever
Sidney Sheldon

In the frenetic world of a big San Francisco hospital, events catapult three women doctors into a white-hot spotlight:

Dr Paige Taylor

She swore it was euthanasia, but when Paige inherited a million dollars from a patient, the District Attorney called it murder.

Dr Kat Hunter

She vowed never to let a man too close again - until she accepted the challenge of a deadly bet.

Dr Honey Taft

To make it in medicine, she knew she'd need something more than the brains God gave her.

Racing from the life and death decisions of the operating room to the tension-packed fireworks of a murder trial, *Nothing Lasts Forever* lays bare the ambitions and fears of healers and killers, lovers and betrayers in a heart-stopping story you wish would never end . . .

'Of all the popular novels I've read this summer this beats the lot for sheer storytelling mastery'   *Today*

0 00 647658 9

Morning, Noon and Night

Sidney Sheldon

The Stanford family is one of the most respected in America - but behind the facade of fame and glamour lies a hidden web of blackmail, drugs and murder . . .

When Harry Stanford, one of the wealthiest men in the world, mysteriously drowns while cruising on his yacht, it sets off a chain of events that reverberates around the globe . . . At the family gathering following the funeral in Boston, a strikingly beautiful young woman appears. She claims to be Stanford's daughter and entitled to a share of the tycoon's estate. Is she genuine or is she an imposter?

Sweeping from the splendours of the Italian Riviera, to the fashion salons of Paris and New York, and the élite opulence of Boston and Florida, *Morning, Noon and Night* twists and turns its way through intrigue, smoke and mirrors to a surprise ending you'll never forget . . .

'Sheldon is a writer working at the height of his power . . . I hung on till the very end'   *New York Times*

ISBN 0 00 649806 X